GARDEN SWEETS

Connie Shelton

Books by Connie Shelton
THE CHARLIE PARKER MYSTERY SERIES

Deadly Gamble
Vacations Can Be Murder
Partnerships Can Be Murder
Small Towns Can Be Murder
Memories Can Be Murder
Honeymoons Can Be Murder
Reunions Can Be Murder
Competition Can Be Murder
Balloons Can Be Murder
Obsessions Can Be Murder
Gossip Can Be Murder
Stardom Can Be Murder

Phantoms Can Be Murder
Buried Secrets Can Be Murder
Legends Can Be Murder
Weddings Can Be Murder
Alibis Can Be Murder
Escapes Can Be Murder
Sweethearts Can Be Murder
Money Can Be Murder
Road Trips Can Be Murder
Cruises Can Be Murder
Deceptions Can Be Murder

Old Bones Can Be Murder - a Halloween novella
Holidays Can Be Murder - a Christmas novella

THE SAMANTHA SWEET SERIES

Sweet Masterpiece
Sweet's Sweets
Sweet Holidays
Sweet Hearts
Bitter Sweet
Sweets Galore
Sweets Begorra
Sweet Payback
Sweet Someethings
Sweets Forgotten

Spooky Sweet
Sticky Sweet
Sweet Magic
Deadly Sweet Dreams
The Ghost of Christmas Sweet
Tricky Sweet
Haunted Sweets
Secret Sweets
Garden Sweets

Spellbound Sweets - a Halloween novella
Thankful Sweets - a Thanksgiving novella
The Woodcarver's Secret - prequel to the series

THE HEIST LADIES SERIES
Diamonds Aren't Forever
The Trophy Wife Exchange
Movie Mogul Mama
Homeless in Heaven
Show Me the Money

CHILDREN'S BOOKS
Daisy and Maisie and the Great Lizard Hunt
Daisy and Maisie and the Lost Kitten

Garden Sweets

Samantha Sweet Mysteries, Book 19

Connie Shelton

Secret Staircase Books

Garden Sweets
Published by Secret Staircase Books, an imprint of
Columbine Publishing Group, LLC
PO Box 416, Angel Fire, NM 87710

Book layout and design by Secret Staircase Books
Cover images © BooksRMe, Anna Komisarenko, Dulsita, RKasprzak
First trade paperback edition: April, 2025
First e-book edition: April, 2025

* * *

Publisher's Cataloging-in-Publication Data

Shelton, Connie
Garden Sweets / by Connie Shelton.
p. cm.
ISBN 978-1649142054 (paperback)
ISBN 978-1649142061 (e-book)

1. Samantha Sweet (Fictitious character)--Fiction. 2. Taos, New
Mexico—Fiction. 3. Paranormal activity—Fiction. 4. Bakery—
Fiction. 5. Women sleuths—Fiction. I. Title

Samantha Sweet Mystery Series.
Shelton, Connie, Samantha Sweet mysteries.

BISAC : FICTION / Mystery & Detective.

813/.54

To you, my readers.
You make this writer's journey so worthwhile.

Chapter 1

Samantha Sweet circled the block, steering her bakery van into the alley behind Sweet's Sweets. Driving the distinctive vehicle with its images of baked goods and the logo of the shop, she'd made the morning deliveries, grabbed some lunch, and was back to tend to the early afternoon crowd. Ivan Petrenko's little car was parked behind his bookshop next door. She noted that Riki Davis-Jones wasn't at her dog grooming shop to the east, since Riki had taken a long weekend to drive to Albuquerque for supplies and a little shopping spree.

Sam reached for the door handle, gathering her bag and baker's jacket, just as her phone rang. Zoë. Her best friend for more years than either of them could remember.

"Hey, what's up?"

"Hey, Sam. I've only got a second, but wanted to ask—

have you heard from Victor Martinez recently? I'm not getting answers to my calls."

Sam paused and took a breath. "Actually, no. Which is kind of weird. He's normally somewhere around here or near the plaza, getting the flower boxes spruced up."

"Yeah. I'm ready to have him come out to the B&B to help me with my spring plantings, and I've got a couple of dead shrubs that need to be taken out and replaced."

"You tried both his home number and his cell?"

"Oh yeah. And I asked Darryl to keep an eye out for his truck. We haven't seen any sign of him."

"I can ask around. Maybe stop by his house."

Zoë sighed over the line. "We've done that. Darryl went by there and says the place looks locked up tight. Victor's truck is there, but it doesn't look like it's been moved in a while. He says Victor's own garden is looking a little untended, too. That's really not like him."

Sam spotted Becky Gurule, her chief decorator, standing in the doorway to the bakery. "I gotta go, Zoë, but I'll ask around, see if anyone else knows anything. I'm swamped this week at the bakery."

"Right. It's Easter really soon. Make me an extra pan of your fabulous hot cross buns this week. We're having new guests coming in on Good Friday. I'll pick up the buns that morning, if that works for you."

"You got it." Sam ended the call and climbed out of her van, greeting Becky as she walked into the Sweet's Sweets kitchen.

The sweet aroma of cinnamon and vanilla surrounded Sam as Becky filled her in on the morning's business. Julio had trays of hot cross buns baked, and more in the oven. Racks and racks of sugar cookies sat on the worktable, awaiting decoration, and Becky was more than halfway done with an elaborate wedding cake.

As they chatted, Sam set her bag aside and slipped her baker's jacket on over her simple clothing. The bells above the front door tinkled, signaling the arrival of customers. Jennifer Baca's voice greeted them in the sales room, the familiar chatter of voices filled the air, a comforting background noise that Sam had come to associate with the heartbeat of her bakery.

"Sounds like Jen's busy already out there," Sam said. "I'll go and quickly check the coffee and tea supplies, and then I'll get busy with the cookie decorations." She stepped through the curtain that separated the sales area and kitchen.

"Hi, Sam!" called out Sophie Hernandez, a regular who always stopped by for her daily coffee and pastry. "The lemon scones are especially light and wonderful today."

Sam smiled, her eyes roaming toward the little bins that held sugar and creamer. "Thanks, Sophie. Can I top off that coffee for you?"

"Zoë Chartrain was just asking about Victor Martinez," she mentioned as she poured the coffee. "Any idea where he is?"

From the next table came the gruff voice of Willie Baca, the retired postmaster. "I haven't seen him around lately. Usually he's out and about, fixing things up for folks this time of year."

"I heard his ex-wife say he went down to Mexico," Sophie chimed in. "Something about visiting family."

Sam felt her skepticism rising. Victor rarely traveled, and he'd never mentioned any family in Mexico.

"Sam? You okay?"

Sam forced a smile, realizing she'd been standing still, holding the coffee carafe aloft, for several moments. "Oh, sorry, just trying to remember if I ordered enough Earl Grey tea for the week."

But as she rearranged tea bags and replenished a container of stir-sticks, she puzzled over the comments about Victor Martinez, like an itch she couldn't scratch, a nagging feeling that there was more to the story.

She turned her attention back to her customers; she could certainly gather more information the old-fashioned way. "So, Mr. Baca," she called out casually, "when *was* the last time you saw Victor?"

"Oh gosh, it was when I saw him heading up the ski valley road. Must've been, what, early December?"

That was months ago. Sam gripped her washcloth as she casually wiped the beverage bar area. The mountains in winter? That didn't sound like Victor at all. He'd always avoided snowy days, preferring to hunker down in town during the coldest winter months.

"Really?" she found herself saying before she could stop herself. "You saw Victor in the mountains?"

The postmaster looked up, surprised. "Why, yes, Ms. Sweet. Spotted him on the road to Taos Ski Valley. Thought it was odd, him being out there on a snowy day."

"Did he say where he was going?"

"No, just waved as he drove by. Seemed in a hurry, now that I think about it."

"Hm, okay. Well, if any of you happen to see him, can you ask him to call Zoë Chartrain at the B&B?"

The bells above the door interrupted Sam's train of thought. She turned to see Kelly breezing in, her red-brown curls bouncing with each step.

"Mom!" Kelly called out, enveloping Sam in a warm hug that smelled of sunshine and wildflowers. "How's the Easter prep going?"

"Oh, you know, the usual chaos," Sam murmured with a chuckle as they walked back toward the kitchen. "But we're managing. How's my favorite granddaughter?"

Kelly grinned. "Ana's been asking when she can come decorate cookies again. I think she's more excited about that than the actual Easter egg hunt!"

"Tell her I can use help anytime." Sam gave a nod toward the worktable filled with cookies.

"Kelly," Sam interjected gently, her voice lowering. "Have you heard anything from Victor Martinez recently? Zoë and Darryl haven't been able to reach him."

Kelly bit her lower lip. "You know, now that you mention it, I haven't seen him since ... gosh, it must have been early winter. Remember that big snowstorm we had?"

Sam nodded, pondering. She'd hoped Kelly might have some more recent news, but this only deepened the mystery. "That long ago? Did he say anything about taking a trip or ..."

Kelly shook her head thoughtfully. "No, nothing like that. He was supposed to come by and help Scott with some repairs on the greenhouse, but he never showed. We figured he got busy with other jobs, but ..." She trailed off. "Mom? You don't think something's happened to him, do you?"

Sam forced a reassuring smile. "I'm sure he's fine, honey. Probably just got caught up in something. You know Victor, always willing to lend a hand wherever it's needed."

"Yeah, probably. Sounds like a mystery that needs

solving, Mom. Right up your alley …"

"Oh, no, no. Not right now. I'm sure he'll turn up. Anyway, there's no use speculating. How about we focus on something we can actually manage?" She gestured to the trays of undecorated cookies cooling on the worktable. "Since you're not working at Puppy Chic today … these Easter bunnies aren't going to frost themselves."

Kelly's face brightened, her green eyes sparkling. "Sure!"

They settled into a comfortable rhythm, Sam piping delicate outlines while Kelly filled them in with pastel-hued royal icing. The familiar scents of the bakery hung in the air, the warm aromas of chocolate, sugar, and Julio's herb-crusted breadsticks.

"Remember how we used to do this, when I was little?" Kelly mused, carefully adding polka dots to a lavender egg. "You'd let me go wild with the sprinkles."

Sam chuckled, her hands steady as she frosted a bunny's ear. "Oh, I remember. You once dumped an entire jar on a single cookie. I was finding those tiny beads in the oddest places around the house for weeks after that."

As they worked, Sam's mind drifted, thinking of her spring flowers. "You know, Victor helped me plant those tulip bulbs in front of the shop last year, the ones that are absolutely gorgeous now. He had this knack for knowing exactly where each color should go."

Kelly nodded, a fond smile playing on her lips. "He does have quite the artistic eye for gardening. Remember how proud he was when those sunflowers he planted for Ana reached taller than the fence?"

"*Sí, pequeña*, they're reaching for the sky, just like you!" Sam said, mimicking Victor's slightly accented English and warm tone. The memory of his ready smile and twinkling eyes as he'd shown Ana the towering flowers brought a bittersweet pang to Sam's chest.

"I miss seeing him around," Kelly said softly, her icing tip hovering over a half-decorated egg. "It's not just the handiwork, you know? It's … him. His stories about the desert animals, the way he'd make up funny voices for them, to make Ana laugh."

Sam reached out, giving her daughter's hand a gentle squeeze. "I know, sweetheart. There has to be a simple explanation. I'll ask around, maybe some of his customers have seen him."

And then there was Joe at the hardware store, she thought. Their handyman friend bought supplies there often. If anyone would know about Victor's recent projects, it'd be him.

"Mom," Kelly said, a hint of amusement in her tone, "I know that look. You're going into sleuth mode, aren't you?"

Sam grimaced. "These next ten days are going to be crazy around here. I really have no time for chasing down someone, just because I haven't seen him around in a while. But …if something's happened to him, we need to know. I'll find out if Beau has heard anything. And if Victor's just … I don't know, taken an impromptu vacation to Acapulco, well, then we can all breathe easy."

But even as she said it, Sam knew in her gut that the answer wouldn't be that simple. Victor Martinez wasn't the type to vacation in exotic locales, and certainly not the type to vanish without a word to anyone. Somebody had to know where he'd gone.

The bell above the front door went off several times

in a row, heralding a fresh wave of customers into Sweet's Sweets. She realized that a couple of hours had slid by while they decorated.

"Kelly, can you help Jen man the register?" Sam asked, organizing the finished cookies.

"On it, Mom!" Kelly replied, springing into action.

Sam carried the tray of finished cookies to the front and watched with pride as her daughter effortlessly engaged with customers, her enthusiasm showing as she described the Easter specials. She and Jen moved in perfect sync.

Back in the kitchen, Becky showed off her results on the wedding cake. "It's gorgeous, Becky. Let me get a box for it, and I'll deliver it on my way home."

"Mom?" Kelly's voice came through. "We're running low on the lemon tarts."

"Right," Sam said, handing a large, open-top box to Becky. As she moved to retrieve more tarts from the walk-in fridge, Sam thought briefly of the carved wooden box on her dresser at home.

"I wonder," Sam murmured to herself as she loaded a tray with lemon tarts, "if I could use my ... gift ... to find out what happened to Victor."

As a last resort, maybe.

"Here we go," Sam announced, emerging from the kitchen. As she arranged the lemon tarts in the display case, she switched her focus.

The bakery buzzed with the cheerful chatter of customers, the clinking of spoons against cups, and the warm aroma of baked goods. A sense of contentment washed over her, momentarily pushing aside her worries.

"You know, Kel," Sam said, turning to her daughter with a soft smile, "days like this remind me why I love this place so much."

Kelly nodded, her eyes twinkling. "It's pretty special, Mom. You've created something amazing here."

Sam's gaze swept across the bakery, taking in the walls adorned with local art, the afternoon shadows through the windows, and the faces of her regulars.

Walking back into the kitchen, Kelly grabbed her bag, ready to head out. "I should get going. Ana's probably driving Scott crazy with her latest 'experiment'."

Sam chuckled, picturing her precocious granddaughter. "Give that little scientist a hug from me, will you?"

"Will do," Kelly said, planting a quick kiss on Sam's cheek. "Love you, Mom. And don't worry too much, okay?"

Sam pulled her daughter into a tight hug, breathing in the familiar scent of the herbal shampoo that always clung to Kelly's curls. "Thanks, sweetie. I appreciate that more than you know. And thanks … for everything."

Watching her daughter drive away, Sam turned her attention to the window displays she had recently updated with Easter decorations. Her eyes drifted to the empty street beyond. "Where are you, Victor?" Now that others had begun talking about him, the absence of his cheerful presence felt like a void in the fabric of their close-knit community.

The last of the customers had left, and as she began to tidy up the tables and chairs, Sam moved mechanically. Julio and Becky had already left for the day; Jen was at the register, running the day's receipts, gathering the money so Sam could make a bank deposit.

"Mrs. Budagher mentioned seeing him at the hardware store," Jen mused aloud, her voice quiet in the empty shop.

"And Tom Fields swears he spotted Victor's truck near the old Martinez place just after Thanksgiving."

"Thanks for keeping your ears open," Sam said, taking the bank bag as the two of them walked out the door, locking up. "Those little observations could be helpful." A memory surfaced—Victor's proud grin as he showed her the tomato plants he'd coaxed to life in her garden last spring.

"'*Es como magia*, Señora Sam,'" she echoed his words, a sad smile tugging at her lips. "It is like magic."

Chapter 2

Sam had intended to ask Beau about Victor, whether anyone had filed a missing person report or if there were rumors around the sheriff's department, but when she arrived at home she realized he'd sent a text. I'll be in Santa Fe at a meeting all evening. Don't wait up. Love you.

She snacked on crackers and cheese, fed the dogs, and took a shower before falling into bed. At some point she was aware of Beau crawling in beside her, but by daylight he was gone again. She saw lights on in the barn and knew he and his ranch hand, Danny, were tackling the morning chores early. She dressed in her bakery attire, then left a note beside the coffee maker before heading out. Another holiday, another busy season, she reminded herself with a sigh. Sometimes, she and her wonderful hubby only connected on a hit-and-miss basis.

The aroma of Julio's cinnamon rolls wafted through Sweet's Sweets as Sam bustled behind the glass display case, carefully arranging a tray of flaky apple turnovers. The morning sunlight filtered through the bakery's windows, casting a warm glow on the adobe walls and highlighting the swirls of steam rising from coffee cups.

"Jen, can you pass me those chocolate croissants?" Sam asked, gesturing to a cooling rack nearby.

"Sure thing, Sam," Jen replied, her dark hair neatly pulled back in its usual bun. She gracefully maneuvered around a customer to grab the pastries.

As Sam placed each croissant in the case with meticulous care, she couldn't help but feel a sense of pride. Sweet's Sweets had become a cornerstone of the town, a place where neighbors gathered to share stories over cups of coffee and muffins, scones, and slices of her homemade cheesecakes. The steady hum of conversation and the occasional clink of a spoon against porcelain created a comforting melody that Sam had come to associate with home.

Mrs. Coppell, a regular customer with silver hair and kind eyes, approached the counter with a warm smile. "Good morning, ladies," she said, her gaze drifting to the cinnamon rolls. "One of those, please. They smell divine."

As Jen rang up the order, she posed the question that was on all their minds, about whether anyone had seen Victor Martinez in recent weeks.

Sam noticed Mrs. Coppell's brow wrinkle slightly. "You know," Mrs. Coppell began, lowering her voice, "he usually tends to my garden in the spring, but I haven't been able to reach him."

Sam wanted answers, but wasn't sure how much to add

to the gossip mill. Careful to keep her tone neutral, she asked, "Did he mention any travel plans to you?"

Mrs. Coppell shook her head, accepting her pastry from Jen. "Not a word. It's not like him to take a vacation."

As Mrs. Coppell moved to find a seat, Sam considered the woman's statement. Victor's reliability was one of his most admirable traits. For him to vanish without a trace seemed completely out of character. She thought back to the last time she'd seen him, fixing some loose trim around the bakery's front window last November. His weathered face had been creased in concentration, as he balanced precariously on the ladder.

It was as if Jen read her mind as her young employee shook her head, her deep brown eyes reflecting Sam's growing concern. "It's weird, right? He's always around, especially this time of year."

Sam nodded, absently wiping down the counter. As she watched the morning crowd chatting and enjoying their pastries, she reminded herself again to ask Beau if he'd heard anything through his sheriff's grapevine, a question that would require more than a quick text. Maybe they'd be able to meet up for lunch.

For now, though, there were customers to serve and a ton of holiday orders to fill. Sam pushed her worries aside, focusing on the task at hand. She would keep asking questions and hope like crazy that someone had the answers.

She paused midway through refilling the coffee urns, picking up a bag of her special signature blend.

Mrs. Coppell caught her attention. "What you asked earlier, about Victor Martinez, I've been thinking. It's the strangest thing. Several of the neighbors on DeVargas

Lane have been wondering the same thing. And Victor's own yard is starting to look a bit unkempt, which isn't like him at all."

Sam was about to ask another question when Mr. Garcia, a portly man with a salt-and-pepper mustache, stepped away from the counter and approached their table.

"Couldn't help but overhear," he said, his eyes crinkling. "You're talking about Victor Martinez, right? The handyman?"

"Yes, that's right," Sam replied. "Have you seen him recently, Mr. Garcia?"

The man shook his head, his expression troubled. "Not since early winter. He came by to fix a leaky roof for me. Did a bang-up job, as always. Even threw in some Spanish swear words when he nearly slipped off the ladder." Mr. Garcia chuckled, then sobered. "But now that you mention it, that is odd. He usually checks in about doing our spring maintenance by now."

What if Victor had met with an accident? But that didn't make sense either. Accidents and illnesses were generally hot topics of conversation around the bakery, especially with the early morning coffee crowd. Surely she would have heard about it. "Did he mention any plans to travel or take time off?" she asked, trying to keep her tone casual.

"*Nada*," Mr. Garcia replied, shaking his head. "He seemed his usual self. Talked about spring planting and some plans he had for the flower boxes around the plaza, if I remember correctly."

Sam stood, leaving the customers to their coffee while she went back into the kitchen to see if Julio had sliced the two freshly baked quiches yet. Something was definitely amiss with this whole thing. For someone who had always been as reliable as the sunrise over Taos Mountain, Victor's suddenly being unavailable was completely out of character.

She picked up the quiche pans and walked out to the sales area, in time to see Ivan Petrenko stroll in, wearing his usual button-down shirt and dark slacks.

"Ah, Samantha! Good morning, *mon dorogaya*!" Ivan called out, as usual, mixing his Russian, French, and English phrases.

Sam couldn't help but smile. "Morning, Ivan. Your normal cup of our signature blend?"

"*Da, pozhaluysta.* Your coffee is better than my babushka's tea, and that's saying something!"

While Sam poured Ivan's drink, she overheard Mr. Garcia mentioning Victor's name again. Ivan's ears perked up like a curious cat's.

"Victor, the handyman, *da*?" Ivan chimed in, leaning on the counter. "I saw the strangest thing yesterday. That Rosalita, the cleaning woman—his ex—was setting an old chair out in front of his house. Very peculiar, no?"

Sam paused in mid-step. "She's clearing out furniture? Are you sure?"

Ivan nodded vigorously. "As sure as I am that Dostoevsky is superior to Tolstoy. Big red sign, offering this item for sale, couldn't miss it."

Sam froze. Victor loved that little adobe house of his and all of his things. He'd often joked about keeping his grandmother's furniture and about being buried in the backyard next to his prized chile plants. And what was his ex-wife doing, clearing out his things? Something was definitely not right.

She set Ivan's mug down and lowered her voice. "Ivan,

did you happen to talk to Rosalita when you saw her putting up the sign?"

Ivan's bushy eyebrows shot up. "*Oui*, actually, I did. She was all smiling, which was odd enough. Said she was managing Victor's affairs while he's 'gallivanting' around Mexico." He snorted. "What is this gallivanting? Victor? That man hasn't left Taos in thirty years!"

Sam's heart sank. This was the second person to mention his being out of the country.

As Ivan sipped his coffee, Sam pondered. The pieces didn't fit. Victor, suddenly traveling, without a word? And Rosalita, who was somewhat known, among her housekeeping clients, for spinning tales that changed faster than the weather—what was she up to?

"It doesn't make sense," Sam muttered.

"What was that, *chérie?*" Ivan asked, peering over his mug.

Sam shook her head, forcing a smile. "Oh, nothing. Just thinking out loud."

She busied herself stacking empty trays, but her attention was far from the task at hand. Rosalita's reputation for being devious was no secret. The woman could charm the rattles off a snake if it suited her purposes.

Foul play? The thought flitted through Sam's mind like a hummingbird, there and gone in an instant. She quickly pushed it aside, not wanting to jump to conclusions. After all, her experiences with the carved box had taught her that things weren't always as they seemed.

"Everything is all right, Samantha?" Ivan's voice broke through her reverie.

Sam pasted on her best baker's smile. "Just wondering what Victor might be up to in Mexico. I hope he's having fun."

As Ivan launched into a story about his own adventures

south of the border, Sam nodded along. For now, she'd keep her suspicions to herself. Maybe she could break away this afternoon to talk with Beau. Meanwhile, she would mention the missing gardener and handyman to everyone who crossed her path.

She turned her attention to the beverage bar, a spot that tended to become disorganized as people helped themselves to hot drinks and spilled granules of sugar everywhere. She methodically restocked the tea canisters, but she kept coming back to the subject at hand.

"Sam, watch the counter. I'm going to see if there are more croissants ready yet," Jen said in a low voice.

"Sure, and could you grab another box of Darjeeling from the back?"

As Jen disappeared into the kitchen, a regular customer approached the counter. "Morning, Sam! How's business?"

Sam smiled warmly, seizing the opportunity. "Good morning, George. Business is great, thanks." She picked up the cranberry scone he pointed to and placed it in a bag. "Say, have you seen Victor Martinez around lately? I've been meaning to ask him about some yard work."

George considered the question for a moment. "Come to think of it, I haven't seen him in weeks. Isn't that odd?"

Sam nodded, somehow not surprised. "It is, isn't it? I hope everything's all right with him."

George nodded in agreement. "Sounds like another mystery for you to solve," he teased.

When Jen returned to take over the sales counter, Sam retreated to her desk at the back of the kitchen. She sank into her chair, pulling out a notepad.

"What do I actually know?" she murmured, jotting down the facts. *Victor's been missing since early winter. Rosalita's selling his furniture, or some of it anyway. He's supposedly in Mexico, although none of us really believe that. I need to turn all this over to Beau, let the sheriff's department take over.*

Her contemplation was interrupted by a high-pitched squeal of delight from the front of the bakery. She rose from her desk, curiosity piqued, and made her way back to the counter.

A little girl, no more than five, was standing on her tiptoes, nose pressed against the display case. Her golden curls bounced as she pointed excitedly at the array of cupcakes, each topped with a swirl of vibrant frosting.

"Mommy, look! They're like rainbows!" the child exclaimed, her eyes wide with wonder.

Sam couldn't help but smile, her worries about Victor momentarily pushed aside. "Which one's your favorite, sweetie?" she asked, crouching down to the girl's eye level.

The little girl stared, concentrating hard. "Um … the blue one! No, the pink! No, wait …" She giggled, clearly overwhelmed by the choices.

Jen, who had been arranging a fresh batch of cookies nearby, caught Sam's eye and grinned. "How about a special treat while you decide?" she suggested, reaching for a chocolate chip cookie.

"Is that okay, Mom?" the child asked, looking up at her mother with pleading eyes.

As the mother nodded her assent, Sam watched Jen hand over the cookie with a flourish. The girl's face lit up with joy, and for a moment, the bakery was filled with nothing but the simple happiness of a child with a sweet treat.

"Thank you!" the little girl chirped, already munching contentedly.

As the pair moved away from the counter, Sam straightened up. She headed back to the kitchen and pulled a large pan of brownies from the cooling rack. While she mixed chocolate buttercream, her mind drifted back to the mystery at hand.

Before I talk to Beau, I could check out Victor's house, she thought, spreading the buttercream over the moist brownies. *If Rosalita's really selling stuff, there might be clues there about what's going on.*

She cut the brownies into generous squares and arranged them on a tray, working automatically. After carrying them out to the sales room, she glanced at the kitchen clock, mentally rearranging her afternoon schedule. *I can swing by after the lunch rush. Maybe I'll catch Rosalita there, or at least get a look around the property.*

She wiped up dabs of the chocolate frosting, placed the mixing bowl in the sink, and picked up the stack of orders from the basket on her desk. Several of the bigger cakes were ready to be delivered. Becky had two birthday cakes finished and ready for customers to pick up, a wedding cake had the rough-coat icing on it and was ready for fondant, and everything else could wait until tomorrow.

"Becky, will it throw a hitch in things if I skip out for a couple hours? I'll make the deliveries first."

Her assistant shook her head. "Go. You're preoccupied about this whole thing with Victor, and you'll rest easier if you're able to find answers."

"True. Maybe I'll run into Rosalita and she can give me a number where he can be reached. A simple phone call might be all it takes. At least I can find out when he's coming back and maybe convince him that a lot of people are ready to pay him for his services."

Becky chuckled. "I've never known you to give up, Sam. Just do it."

Sam stepped into the walk-in fridge and started pulling out the cakes to be delivered. As she mentally mapped out her route, she pictured the people behind each order—the Johnsons' 50th anniversary, Terry Garcia's quinceañera, old Mr. Wilkins' surprise party. She could stop by Victor's place on her route, just to take a look. If he'd taken a little trip, maybe he was back by now and the whole mystery would be solved.

"You know, Becky," Sam said, looking up at her head decorator, "sometimes I think we're delivering more than just cakes. We're part of people's stories, their memories."

Becky nodded, carefully boxing up a three-tiered chocolate masterpiece. "That's what I love about this job. It's like we're woven into the fabric of Taos."

"And when a thread goes missing, it affects us all."

"You're thinking about Victor again, aren't you?" Jen asked, walking into the kitchen. She picked up one of the boxed cakes and opened the back door to access Sam's delivery van.

"I can't help it," Sam admitted as she sorted the order sheets. "He's been part of this town for so long. It just doesn't sit right, him vanishing like this."

She picked up her bag and carried the quinceañera cake to the back door. "I'm going to find out what's going on."

"Good for you. Everyone trusts that you'll figure it out. But, just be careful, Sam," Jen cautioned. "You remember what happened last time you got mixed up in—"

"I know, I know," Sam interrupted with a wry smile. "But I can't just sit back and do nothing. Not when it comes to one of our own."

With a final nod to her crew, Sam gathered her keys and headed for the door. She paused for a moment as a fresh breeze whooshed down the alley.

Everyone trusts you to figure this out.

Right. When I find the time.

In her delivery van, Sam pulled out of the alley, making the turn onto Don Fernando Street, forcing herself to focus on her driving and the fragile cargo in the van, at least until the deliveries were done and she could turn back to her investigation.

Chapter 3

She began with the delivery farthest from the bakery, the fellowship hall at the Baptist church where the Johnson's anniversary party would take place this evening. A pleasant woman from the kitchen greeted her and showed her where to set up the cake.

Next up, Sam drove over to Lambert's, the restaurant near the plaza, where the quinceañera party had apparently booked the whole place. Marveling at the elaborate decorations, she left the multi-tiered cake with the party planner and was on her way in under five minutes.

Victor Martinez's home was on a side street to the east of the plaza, only a few blocks away, so she headed that direction, hoping she would remember the exact address. That part of it turned out to be easier than expected— Victor's ancient pickup truck sat in the driveway. Good—

maybe he was home.

But as she parked and walked up to the front door, it was clear that he wasn't. The truck had a heavy layer of dust and winter grime, and Sam knew the local gardener took pride in keeping his vehicle clean, even though it was old and a little beat up. Plus, there was a layer of dust and dried-up leaves on the front porch. She knocked at the door anyway, but wasn't surprised when there was no response.

Her eyes scanned the yard, noting the unmown patch of lawn and stalks of plants that he would have cleared away weeks ago. Hm. Maybe the rumors were true and their favorite garden expert had gone away. She debated walking around back to see if she could learn more, but the third cake wouldn't be in great shape if she left it in the van too long. She turned away and left to make her final delivery. The Wilkins surprise party was farther south, in a nice little development out near the hospital, and the young woman who answered the door happily exclaimed over the cake Becky had created for them.

When she walked back into Sweet's Sweets, Becky greeted her with a question about an order she was working on. "I see that we promised these cupcakes would be done in those bunny-shaped molds, and I can't find them on the shelf."

"Let me check the other storeroom. It's been at least a year since we used those." Sam pulled out her key ring and walked outside to access the seldom-used storage space at the back of the building.

Her footsteps echoed softly against the worn wooden floor as she navigated the cluttered storeroom. Shelves lined with baking supplies and miscellaneous items stretched before her, casting long shadows in the dim light filtering through the open door. Her eyes scanned methodically, searching for the misplaced pastry molds.

"Now where did I put those?" she muttered, pushing aside a stack of napkin packets.

As she looked behind a precarious tower of cake pans, something caught her eye. Tucked away in a shadowy corner, partially obscured by a fallen apron, sat a red toolbox, not hers.

"What on earth …?"

She knelt down, her knees protesting slightly—a reminder of her fifty-plus years. With a tentative hand, she brushed away a thin layer of dust from the toolbox's surface. The gritty texture beneath her fingertips sent a shiver of unease through her.

"How long has this been here?" she wondered aloud.

Images of Victor's cheerful face flashed through her memory. His last visit to Sweet's Sweets had been almost five months ago, just as winter was setting in. He'd fixed a leaky faucet, his usual efficiency tempered by easy conversation peppered with Spanish phrases she'd come to find endearing. She remembered him saying something about leaving the tools here until they were sure the leak was fixed. She'd expected him back within a day or two, but then in the Thanksgiving and Christmas rush she'd completely forgotten.

Sam's hand hovered over the toolbox's latch. A part of her hesitated, feeling like she shouldn't be going through his things. But the mystery of his disappearance overrode her reservations. Maybe he'd written down a schedule of his appointments and she could figure out where he'd planned to go after he finished her job. It would at least give her someplace to start in creating a timeline of his activities.

"Sorry, Victor," she whispered, "but we're all just a little bit worried about you."

She flipped open the latch, and lifted the toolbox lid, the familiar scent of metal and oil wafting up, stirring memories of Victor's countless repairs around her bakery.

"Let's see what we've got here," she murmured, methodically inspecting the contents.

She brushed past screwdrivers and pliers, each neatly arranged in its designated spot. Victor's orderliness had always impressed her. As she moved a set of wrenches, a flash of white caught her eye. Tucked beneath the tools, lay a crumpled piece of paper.

Sam's heart quickened. "Maybe a schedule?"

Carefully, she extracted the note, unfolding it. The handwriting was not his, and it looked hurried and scrawled: *It's a fair price, so don't be stupid about this. You in?*

A 'fair price' could refer to any of his jobs, a quote he'd given someone. But the question posed in the note, and the tone. That didn't sound like a bid reference. And the fact that the note was wadded up sort of suggested that he hadn't wanted to deal with it. What had Victor gotten himself into?

"Strange," Sam muttered, studying the cryptic message. "You've always been so open, so ..." She trailed off, recalling Victor's easy smile and willingness to lend a hand to anyone in need.

Don't be stupid about this. Who would say that to their gardener?

The spring breeze drifting through the storeroom's open door suddenly felt chilly. Sam glanced around, half-expecting to see shadowy creatures lurking in the corners. She shook her head, chiding herself for letting her imagination run wild.

"Get a grip, Samantha," she told herself firmly. "There's got to be a logical explanation for this."

But even as she tried to rationalize the situation, Sam couldn't shake the feeling that Victor's disappearance was far more complex—and potentially dangerous—than anyone had initially thought. Her protective nature, honed by years of being around her law-enforcement husband, kicked into high gear. It was definitely time to share this with him.

"Whatever's going on," she vowed, carefully flattening and folding the note, slipping it into her pocket, "I'm going to get to the bottom of it."

She found the bunny molds for Becky, her footsteps echoing softly against the wooden floor as she exited the storeroom. She set the dusty pastry molds in the kitchen sink and told Becky and Julio she had an errand.

The short walk to the sheriff's office was a blur of adobe buildings and deep blue sky, but Sam's mind felt too preoccupied to fully appreciate the mild spring weather. She went to the back door, the one used by Beau and his deputies, and entered the keypad code she remembered from the past. As she pulled open the heavy door, the familiar scent of coffee and the low hum of conversation washed over her.

"Hey there, Sam," Deputy Rico called out, his face crinkling into a smile. "Brought us any of those famous brownies?"

"Oh, not today, Rico," Sam replied, thinking she easily could have brought the guys a treat. "Maybe next time. Is Beau in?"

Deputy Walters, hunched over a stack of paperwork,

looked up. "Sure is. Go on back."

Sam nodded her thanks, then hesitated at Beau's office door. She rapped her knuckles against the door. "Beau? Got a minute?"

Beau glanced up from the case files spread across his desk, his expression softening as he saw her. "For you? Always. What's on your mind, sweetheart?"

Sam stepped inside, closing the door behind her. He had new lines around his eyes, and she hoped that coming back to the top job in the department hadn't proven to be more than he wanted. She walked over to his side and kissed his temple before taking a seat across from him.

"I hope I'm not overreacting, and maybe this is all some misunderstanding, but …"

"Sam? Just say it."

"So, we may have a situation with a missing person." She gave him a brief rundown of the comments she'd heard yesterday and this morning at the bakery. "And then I found something in Victor's toolbox. I think … It sounds like he might be in trouble, Beau."

Sam carefully pulled the crumpled note from her pocket and placed it on Beau's desk. "It was hidden under his tools. I know I shouldn't have been snooping, but … "

Beau frowned as he read the cryptic message aloud. "'Don't be stupid. You in?' What's this about, Sam?"

"I don't know, but it doesn't sound good. No one I've talked to has seen Victor for weeks now, maybe months. This note doesn't sound like it relates to his normal business. It feels like a threat. And now, maybe he's running from something. Or someone."

Beau's expression went from curiosity to apprehension as he considered the implications. He ran a hand through his graying hair, a habit Sam knew meant he was deep in thought.

"The people who were asking about him … were any of them strangers?" Beau asked, his tone shifting to that of the seasoned sheriff.

Sam shook her head. "Just regulars at the bakery. I know most of them, at least by sight."

Beau stood up, moving around the desk to stand beside her. With both hands on her shoulders, he met her gaze. "We'll look into it, Sam. I promise. This note might be cause for concern, but let's not jump to conclusions just yet. It could be nothing."

"True. It's definitely not Victor's handwriting. Could just be a scrap of paper he picked up somewhere."

"Look, you're concerned. And it sounds like others are, too." Beau's voice was steady, grounding her. "First, we'll check to see if there's been a formal missing person report."

He moved back to his chair and wiggled the computer mouse to wake up his terminal. After a few clicks, he squinted at the screen then shook his head. "Nothing on file. I'll have the deputies discreetly ask around town, see if they can locate him. There could be a perfectly logical explanation."

She nodded her thanks and stood up to leave. He met her before she reached the door.

"And Sam?" He gently tilted her chin up to meet his gaze. "I need you to be careful. If Victor really *is* in trouble, we don't know who might be involved."

Sam nodded. "I'll keep my eyes open. You know me, Beau. I can handle myself."

A small smile tugged at Beau's lips. "That's what worries me, sweetheart. Just promise me you won't go playing detective on your own this time?"

"As if I have the time right now." But then she hesitated, knowing full well she couldn't make that promise. Instead, she stretched up and kissed his cheek. "I'll be careful. And I'll let you know if I find anything else."

"Same here." He walked her to the door, a protective hand against her lower back.

As she walked back toward Sweet's Sweets, she had the feeling that the note, the dusty pickup truck, the overgrown gardens … it all pointed to a mystery that was far from over. Beau could send out deputies, but there was something Sam could do, something he didn't fully know about. She got into her van and headed left on Paseo del Pueblo Norte, toward Kelly's house.

Chapter 4

Sam pulled her van under the portico at the side door to the large Victorian. Walking in, she found her daughter in the sunlit kitchen, her cinnamon-colored curls pulled back into an untidy knot at the top of her head. The scent of chamomile drifted upward as she expertly poured steaming water into a teapot.

"Mom!" Kelly's face lit up, but her smile faltered as she caught Sam's expression. "What's wrong?"

Sam sank into a chair at the rustic wooden table, running a hand over her spiky gray hair, the new haircut that still felt strange to her. "I found a note hidden in Victor's toolbox. Kelly, I think he might be in some kind of trouble."

Kelly's eyes widened as she set two mugs of herbal tea on the table, sliding one toward her mother. "Tell me everything," she urged, leaning forward.

Sam recounted her discovery and the meeting with Beau, and she couldn't help but notice the wheels turning behind Kelly's attentive gaze. Her daughter had always been intuitive, quick to pick up on the subtle threads that often eluded others.

"His house unoccupied and his truck dirty? This doesn't sound like Victor at all," Kelly mused. "But no one has reported him missing? He has family in town, doesn't he?"

"His ex-wife, Rosalita. And someone mentioned a nephew … cousin … somebody like that."

Kelly nibbled at her lower lip. "He's always been such a regular guy. For him to be involved in anything … well, anything where someone would threaten him … that's just weird."

Sam nodded, wrapping her hands around the warm mug. "Right? That's what's got me a little on edge. Victor's more than just a handyman and gardener; he's a friend to half the town. And yet, no one thought to report him missing, to go by the house and check on him?"

Kelly was quiet for a moment, her eyes unfocused as if seeing beyond the cozy kitchen. When she spoke, her voice was soft. "Mom, what if we consulted the rune book? It's helped us before when we've hit dead ends."

Sam felt a familiar tug of hesitation. The book of runes had indeed guided them through past mysteries, but it also represented a part of their lives they kept carefully hidden from even their closest friends. "I don't know, Kel. We don't even know if there's anything … sinister about Victor's disappearance yet."

"But that's just it," Kelly pressed gently. "The book might give us a clue about where to start looking. We don't have to tell anyone else, but if it could help find him …"

Sam sighed, torn between her practical nature and the undeniable pull of the mystical tool that had become such an integral part of their lives. "You're right," she conceded finally. "We owe it to Victor to use every resource we have. Even if it means stepping into territory Beau wouldn't exactly approve of."

A small, conspiratorial smile played on Kelly's lips. "He married you knowing full well you can't resist a good mystery, paranormal or otherwise. Now, let's see what the runes have to say about our missing friend."

They carried their tea mugs and climbed the narrow stairs to the third-floor attic, with Eliza the calico cat slipping past to go with them.

Sam inhaled deeply as she entered, the familiar scent of aged wood and pungent herbs filling her lungs. Soft light streamed through the bay window, casting a warm glow over the cozy space and illuminating motes of dust that danced in the air.

"It always feels like stepping into another time up here," Samantha mused, her eyes roaming over the shadowy corners filled with shelves of books and little bottles, the contents of which they'd never fully explored. The home's former owner had a fascinatingly obscure history.

Kelly nodded. "I know what you mean. It's like the past is alive in this room."

Sam settled at the long table, and Kelly pulled out the artifacts that had become central to their investigations: a carved wooden box nearly identical to the one Sam owned and an ancient leatherbound book filled with strange symbols and drawings.

Her heart quickened with anticipation as she placed

Kelly's carved wooden box between them. Her hands brushed over its surface, following the curved pattern she knew by heart.

"Ready?" Kelly asked, reaching for the book of runes.

Samantha nodded, feeling the familiar tingle of energy that signaled the awakening of her abilities. She gave a quick nod.

As Kelly opened the ancient tome, its pages whispered with secrets of the past. She let the book fall open to a random page. Samantha watched, mesmerized, as her daughter's eyes scanned the symbols.

"It's strange," Samantha said softly. "A few years ago, I would have laughed at the idea of reading runes or sensing auras. Now look at us."

Kelly looked up, a gentle smile on her face. "Life has a way of surprising us, doesn't it, Mom?"

Samantha nodded, contemplating her journey from skepticism to acceptance. She remembered the first time she'd held the box, the shock of realizing she could see things others couldn't. It had been terrifying, exhilarating, and utterly life-changing.

"No matter how often I do this, I still hope we're using these gifts responsibly," Samantha murmured. "There's so much we don't understand."

"We're doing our best," Kelly reassured her, reaching out to squeeze her hand. "And we're helping people. That's what matters."

Samantha smiled, grateful for her daughter's support. As Kelly returned to the runes, Samantha's gaze drifted to the window where Eliza sat on the window seat, attentive to their actions. The familiar view toward Taos Mountain grounded her, a reminder of the real world beyond this attic of mysteries and magic.

"Okay," Kelly said suddenly, her voice filled with excitement and apprehension. "I think I've found something. Are you ready to hear what the runes have to say?"

Sam brought her attention back to the page. "Tell me."

Kelly stared at the intricate symbols on the worn parchment. "The rune for deception is prominent," she murmured, her voice barely above a whisper. "It's intertwined with ... yes, the symbol for hidden truths."

Samantha studied the ancient markings. The familiar scent of aged paper mingled with the dusty attic air, grounding her in the moment.

"What do you think it means?" Samantha asked, her voice tight with anticipation.

Kelly's gaze met her mother's. "I think someone in Taos is hiding something big, Mom. Something that could change everything."

Samantha sat back. "Do you see anything specific to Victor? Anything that tells us the reading is about a gardener or a handyman?"

Kelly shook her head. "You know how it works, Mom. These runes ... they're powerful, but vague. Still, you have to admit, they've never steered us wrong before."

True. She remembered a time when she would have scoffed at the idea of magical runes guiding an investigation. Now, here she was, relying on ancient symbols and her own inexplicable abilities to solve mysteries.

"It's just ..." Samantha paused, searching for the right words.

"What if we're meddling in things we shouldn't? What if we uncover something that puts us in danger?" Kelly reached across the table, squeezing her mother's hand. "That's always been a risk, Mom. Even without the help of the boxes and the runes. But we've helped so many people. Isn't that worth it?"

Samantha nodded slowly. "You're right. We can't ignore this. But we need to be smart about it."

"Agreed," Kelly said, a mischievous glint in her eye. "So, where do we start, Detective Sweet?"

Samantha couldn't help but smile at her daughter's enthusiasm. "Well, first things first. Some interviews, a little poking around, following any leads that come up. But we need to be really careful until we get some idea who we're dealing with."

Kelly's curly cinnamon hair caught the soft light from the bay window. "Mom, I understand your hesitance, but think about it. These runes, they're like a secret language only we can understand. It's not just about solving mysteries; it's about uncovering truths that might never see the light of day otherwise."

Again, Samantha felt a familiar tingle of energy coursing through her as she touched the smooth carvings on the box.

"That's why we're both doing this," Kelly's tone was light but sincere. "Two heads are better than one, especially when they're as stubborn as ours."

Before Samantha could respond, a tap sounded at the door and it creaked open. Kelly discreetly slid the book and box aside. Scott Porter's tall figure filled the doorway, his presence immediately grounding the ethereal atmosphere of their makeshift investigation room.

"Ladies," he said, raising an eyebrow as he surveyed the scene. "Ana's asking what's for dinner. I thought I'd check on our resident sleuths first. I assume that's what you're doing locked away up here?"

Kelly gave him the glossed-over version, just the fact that Victor Martinez appeared to be missing and they were looking for answers. Sam watched her son-in-law's expression carefully, noting the familiar skepticism that flitted across his features.

"Deceit and hidden truths, huh?" Scott mused, pursing his mouth. "Sounds like the plot of my next kids' mystery book. Are you sure this isn't just … well, wishful thinking?"

Samantha felt a flicker of defensiveness. "Scott, we can't ignore the rumors that are flying around town."

"I'm not saying ignore them," Scott said, his tone gentle but firm. "I just don't want you two getting in over your heads."

"We'll be careful," Kelly assured him, reaching out to squeeze his hand. "Promise."

"I understand you're both into feelings and intuition and all, but what about something more concrete? A missing persons report, suspicious activity … anything that isn't based on mystical stuff?"

Samantha explained she'd already checked the records with Beau.

"Hon, we get it," Kelly said, her tone softening.

Samantha nodded, adding, "We're not jumping to conclusions, Scott. But we can't ignore the fact a friend is missing." She thought of the note and its implied threat. "There could be something brewing in town that we need to be aware of."

She paused, considering her next words carefully. "What if … what if someone in our nearby circle is hiding something? Something that affects us all."

Kelly's expression became serious. "Mom's right. We've lived here long enough to know that even in a place as beautiful as Taos, people have secrets."

As they spoke, Samantha's mind zipped through the possibilities. Who in this little town might be concealing a truth so significant that the runes would warn about it? And who might have it in for Victor Martinez? The thought sent a shiver through her, despite the warmth of the attic.

"Look," Scott said, his voice pulling Samantha back to the conversation, "I'm not dismissing your concerns. I just want you both to be careful. Promise me you won't do anything rash?"

Sam nodded, feeling a surge of affection for her son-in-law's protective nature. "We promise, Scott. We'll keep our eyes open and our heads down."

"I should go check on Ana," Scott said, breaking the momentary silence. "She's probably wondering where we've all disappeared to."

As he turned to leave, Sam caught Kelly's eye. A silent understanding passed between them, and Sam cleared her throat. "Scott, wait," she called softly.

He paused at the top of the attic stairs, looking back expectantly.

"I think … I think it's best if we keep this to ourselves for now, just we three and Beau," Samantha said, her voice low. "I mean the runes, the warnings—all of this."

Kelly nodded in agreement. "We don't want to cause unnecessary panic or draw attention to … well, you know." She gestured vaguely at the box and book of runes.

Samantha felt a familiar twinge of unease. How would their neighbors react if they knew about their abilities? Would they be seen as frauds? Or worse, as threats? They'd taken great care not to discuss any of this with outsiders, and it needed to stay that way.

"Oh, absolutely," Scott agreed, his expression softening. "I won't say a word. But promise me you'll be careful, both of you."

"We always are," Kelly assured him with a tight smile.

As Scott's footsteps faded down the stairs, Samantha turned to her daughter. "Kel, we need to tread lightly here. If there's really some huge sham in Taos like the runes suggest …"

Kelly finished her thought, "We could be opening a can of worms we're not prepared for."

Samantha nodded, preoccupied, as she stood and gathered her things. Whatever secrets lay hidden in their picturesque town, she knew they'd have to proceed with caution. The last thing they needed was for their own secrets to be exposed in the process.

"It'll be fine," she assured her daughter. "We'll talk soon."

Downstairs, she scooped up Ana in a big hug, laughing when she saw that Scott and her granddaughter had started making mac and cheese.

"Leave it to a kid to choose the dinner plan, and this is what we get," Kelly joked, tousling her daughter's curly red hair.

Sam distributed kisses all around and headed home in her van. By the time Beau walked into the kitchen of their spacious log home, an hour later, the scent of green chile stew filled the air.

"Do I have time for a shower?" he asked, planting a kiss on her cheek.

"Absolutely. Stew waits for anyone, and the longer it

cooks the better it tastes." She chuckled as she stirred the pot.

"Beau," Samantha began, dishing up bowls of the hearty mixture thirty minutes later, "did your guys have a chance to go out to Victor's house, take a look around?"

Beau shook his head, carrying their bowls to the table. "Yeah, but it was just as you said. No sign of him, Sam. But, based on what we know, it's not really a matter for law enforcement. A guy can leave town without having to report to anyone."

"So, it's okay for me to keep asking around?"

"Sure. Go for it."

Samantha took a deep breath. "Kelly and I did a little …" She waggled her hand to indicate the paranormal activity that he didn't exactly believe in. "We received some warnings from it."

She watched as Beau's eyebrows rose, skepticism clear in his eyes. Yet, his voice remained gentle. "Warnings? About what exactly?"

"Deception, hidden truths," Samantha explained, her voice low. "I know it sounds crazy, but after everything we've seen…"

Beau met her gaze, straight on. "I can't say I fully understand all this, Sam, but I trust you. Both of you." He placed a reassuring hand on hers. "I'll keep an eye out for anything unusual that might back up these warnings. You know you have my support, always."

Samantha felt a wave of relief wash over her. "Thank you," she whispered, leaning into his touch. The blend of professionalism and love in Beau's tone reminded her why she'd fallen for him in the first place.

Later that evening, Samantha slipped into bed beside

Beau, the soft glow of the bedside lamp casting long shadows across their log-walled bedroom. Outside, the deep black of the star-filled Taos night sky pressed against the window, a reminder of the vastness of the mystery they faced.

"I can practically hear your mind working overtime …" Beau murmured, his voice a low rumble in the quiet room. "Just remember, you're not alone in this, and I want you to call me the minute you find anything that might mean someone has broken the law."

Sam settled into the familiar warmth of their bed, unable to ignore the anticipation tingling along her spine. The upcoming, busy Easter week meant she might need to wake up extra early and make use of the energy from the carved box, in order to get her bakery work done and still have time to get out and ask questions. But she could not— would not—leave the mystery of Victor's disappearance alone until she had satisfactory answers.

"Goodnight, Beau," she whispered, squeezing his hand.

"Goodnight, darlin'," he replied, switching off the lamp.

Chapter 5

Samantha's silver-flecked hair caught the sunlight as she strode up the sidewalk to Victor Martinez's adobe home. She felt proud that she'd followed through on her idea from last night, drawing energy from the carved box before heading to Sweet's Sweets, and accomplishing an amazing amount of work before the rest of her crew showed up. Sometimes Julio came in on these mornings and gave her the side-eye, probably wondering if she used some kind of uppers or speed to work so fast. Becky most likely assumed, as a mother of two rambunctious boys, that all women had super powers when it came to time management.

No matter. The main thing was that the bakery was ready to go for the day, and Sam could get out and start looking for leads to find Victor. Her involvement wasn't purely unselfish, she reminded herself—her own property and those of her friends were beginning to desperately need tending.

Now, her keen eyes scanned Victor's property, noting details she'd missed on her previous quick visit. Aside from the overgrown lawn and the weeds pushing through cracks in the walkway, she saw that Victor's prized rose bushes, normally bursting with vibrant blooms this time of year, looked droopy. The flower beds were choked with weeds, and the carefully tended vegetable patch was nothing but withered vines and rotting produce from last fall.

Despite the quiet, there was an unfamiliar white Nissan parked at the curb. Someone must be here.

The neglect seemed glaringly apparent now that the old neighborhood had become somewhat gentrified, with wealthy people snapping up the modest homes and transforming them into showplaces.

"This isn't like Victor at all," Sam muttered. She recalled his pride in his property, the home that had been in his family for many generations.

As she approached the weathered front door, Sam took a breath. She raised her hand and rapped her knuckles against the wood, the sound echoing in the eerie stillness of the property.

She knocked again, harder this time. *Maybe I should try to …* No, Sam shook her head, pushing away the thought of her expertise with lock picks. *Not yet. Let's stick to good old-fashioned detective work for now.*

She stepped back from the door. With one last look at the silent house, Sam turned and started back down the path. Okay, maybe it was time for the lock picks to come out. She could get them from home and come right back.

Just then, the door creaked open, and Sam saw it was Rosalita Suarez y Martinez, Victor's ex. Her face, framed by obviously dyed black hair, lit up with an artificial warmth that quickly morphed into guarded suspicion as she recognized Samantha.

"Señora Sweet," Rosalita said, a gold tooth glinting in the sunlight. "What a surprise. How can I help you today?"

Sam noticed the woman didn't make a move to invite her inside. *Play it as naturally as possible, Sam.*

Sam plastered on her most disarming smile, the one she usually reserved for difficult customers at Sweet's Sweets. "Hi, Rosalita. I hope I'm not interrupting anything. I was just in the neighborhood and thought I'd stop by to check on Victor. Is he around?"

Rosalita seemed to tense, her arms crossing over her chest. "Ah, Victor. No, he's not here right now. I only stopped by to check on the house. He's in Sonora, getting medical treatment. Very sudden, you understand. But necessary."

"Oh! I'm sorry to hear Victor's unwell," Sam said. Could the explanation actually be this simple? "It must have been quite serious for him to leave so suddenly. What is he being treated for?"

Rosalita's earlier smoothness giving way to a hint of irritation. "It ... complicated. The doctors in Sonora are specialists. Victor didn't want to worry anyone."

Sam pressed gently. "But surely his friends here would want to know. When did he leave? How long will he be gone?"

"Ay, so many questions!" Rosalita exclaimed, forcing a laugh that didn't reach her eyes. "He left ... oh, a month ago? Maybe more. You know how time flies. And the treatment, it takes as long as it takes."

A month ago? That didn't fit at all with what others had said.

Sam nodded, ignoring the vague answers and noting a faint yellow aura surrounding the woman. "Of course. I just hope he's getting the care he needs. Victor's always been around. It's not like him to leave without a word."

Rosalita's eyes flashed. "Are you saying I'm lying? Victor trusts me to handle things. That's all you need to know."

"No, no," Sam backpedaled, holding up her hands. "I'm just thinking about a friend. We all are. Is there any way we can send him a card or something?"

"I told you, he needs rest," Rosalita snapped, then visibly composed herself. "But ... I'll let him know people are asking after him. Now, if you'll excuse me, I have things to do."

As Rosalita took a step back, Sam felt that she was about to be shut out of more than just Victor's house. She stepped forward again.

"I appreciate you taking the time to talk with me," Sam said, her voice deliberately casual. She coughed discreetly, buying a moment to consider her next move. "It must be a lot of work, managing everything while Victor's away. His landscaping business, the house ..."

Rosalita's chin lifted, a glint of pride—or was it defensiveness?—in her eyes. "*Sí*, I handle it all with a power of attorney. Victor trusts me completely. The business runs smoothly, bills are paid. Everything is as it should be."

Sam nodded. "That's impressive. Victor's always had such a personal touch with his clients. How are you managing the scheduling and customer preferences?"

The woman's nails tapped an erratic rhythm on the door frame, her gaze darting between Sam's face and a point just over her left shoulder. There was a tension in her shoulders that hadn't been there moments before, as if she was bracing for an attack.

A flicker of uncertainty crossed Rosalita's face before she rallied. "I have his notes, his phone. It's not so difficult." She waved dismissively, but Sam noticed she now clenched the edge of the door tightly.

"Okay," Sam murmured. Something about this didn't add up, but she couldn't quite put her finger on what. She thought of the carved wooden box at home, its effects from this morning wearing off. "And the spring planting season is coming up. A few people told me they've tried to call his number and aren't getting an answer."

Rosalita's eyes flashed, her mood going from defensive to combative in an instant. "What are you implying?" she snapped, her voice rising. "You think I cannot handle such things? That I am not smart enough?"

Sam kept her tone even, despite the tension crackling between them. "Not at all. I'm just curious about the timing, given how sudden Victor's departure seems to have been. And someone mentioned some furniture being sold?"

"It is not your business!" Rosalita hissed, almost baring her teeth. "I am his wife. Who else should be trusted with his affairs?"

Ex-wife, Sam thought. And there might be several people in town more trustworthy than this one.

For a moment, Sam thought Rosalita might actually lunge at her. But just as quickly as it had appeared, the anger drained from Rosalita's face, replaced by a tense smile.

"Forgive me," Rosalita said, her voice honey-sweet once more. "It has been … stressful, managing everything alone."

Sam nodded, realizing that antagonizing the woman wasn't going to help. "I can only imagine. Victor's always been so capable, so involved in everything. It must be hard not having him here. If you'd like to give me his number in Mexico, I could call and offer our assistance with—"

"No!" Rosalita's response was too quick, too sharp. She stopped, visibly composing herself. "I mean, it is not necessary. He needs rest, not distractions."

Sam nodded slowly, filing away every nuance of Rosalita's reactions. "All right, then. Well, thank you for your time, Rosalita. I hope Victor recovers quickly."

As she turned to leave, Sam had a feeling that she'd just stepped into something far more complicated—and potentially dangerous—than she'd dreamed.

Sam stepped off the porch, then paused, turning back. "Oh, one last thing, Rosalita. If you hear from Victor, would you mind letting him know that Beau and I are thinking of him? We'd love to catch up when he's feeling better."

Rosalita's eyes narrowed almost imperceptibly at the mention of the sheriff. "*Sí*, of course. I will tell him."

"Thanks so much," Sam said, struggling to keep her tone light. She waved and started walking toward her van.

"Well, that was interesting," Sam muttered to herself, glancing back at the house. Rosalita was still watching from the doorway, her stocky figure silhouetted against the dim interior, the yellow aura gone now.

Sam climbed into her van, her mind filled with questions. If Victor had left, why was his truck still here? And why go all the way to Mexico—there was excellent medical care as close as Santa Fe or Albuquerque. But, okay, even if the part about medical treatment was true, maybe someone had driven him—all the way to Mexico?—or maybe he'd flown there? And Rosalita's hedging about how long he'd been gone … Sam would definitely have to find out more about that. From the people she'd spoken to, no one had seen him in at least four months.

"Okay, Victor," she said softly as she started the engine. "Where are you really? And what is Rosalita trying to hide?"

As she left the quiet neighborhood, she pondered what she'd learned. Something about this situation felt different, more dangerous perhaps. Sam shook her head, trying to dispel her growing sense of unease.

Chapter 6

Her early morning awakening was catching up with her and Sam realized she really needed solid food. She headed toward one of her favorite places.

The glass door whooshed shut as Sam stepped inside, the aroma of green chile and warm tortilla chips enveloping her. She paused, her eyes scanning the familiar adobe-walled interior at El Taoseño, taking in the crowded tables where patrons sat hunched over steaming food. Lively conversations reached her ears, punctuated by the clink of silverware against plates.

Sam's gaze settled on a familiar figure in loose cotton pants and a billowy tunic, a dash of his signature purple in the form of a scarf over one shoulder. Her friend Rupert Penrick was seated with a woman who had long, dark hair cascading down her back. She was about to request a table for one when Rupert spotted her and signaled her over. She left the smiling hostess behind and wound her way through the tables.

"Sam, come meet Novelle Rojas, artist and sculptor extraordinaire." Rupert stood and grabbed her in one of his lovely bear hugs. "I'm just here to get my takeout order, and I'm afraid I interrupted Novelle's creative time."

He turned toward the seated woman. Sam noticed she had a sketchpad and pencils, which she quickly pushed to the side.

"Novelle, I'm happy to meet you. I've heard of your work for years now."

The slender woman blushed a little.

"Sam, Zoë told me you are both looking for Victor Martinez," Rupert said, out of the blue. "I can ask around, but I haven't personally seen him, and I tell you, my flower garden misses him drastically."

Just then, a server appeared with both hands full. Rupert's order was evidently in the bag she had looped over her fingers, while her right hand gripped a small plate with a simple ham sandwich on it. She set the plate in front of Novelle and handed the bag to Rupert.

"Ladies, this has been so nice, but I must leave you. I promised I would eat at my keyboard today. A writer's work is never done." Rupert fluttered away before either woman could react.

Novelle looked up at Sam and around the crowded room. "You might as well sit."

Sam slid into the seat across from her, nodding toward the sketchpad. "Working on a new piece?"

"Just sketching ideas," Novelle replied, picking up her sandwich while the server took Sam's order for three tacos, to go.

"Anything exciting?" Sam probed, feeling awkward about her enforced intrusion on someone else's lunch.

Novelle shrugged. "Maybe. It's still in the conceptual phase."

Sam nodded. "I haven't seen much of your work lately. Been busy with commissions?"

"Not really," Novelle said, her tone clipped. "The art market's been slow. Unlike some people, I can't rely on steady handyman work to pay the bills."

"Ah. Victor. I don't suppose you've seen him around lately? I've been trying to reach him for some repairs at the bakery."

Novelle's face darkened. "Victor? That jerk owes me money. Borrowed two hundred bucks, months ago, and never paid me back."

Sam's eyebrows rose. This was new information. "Really? That doesn't sound like Victor. He's always been so reliable."

"Well, he wasn't this time," Novelle snapped. "I needed that cash for supplies. Now I'm behind on my work because of him. He's a creative guy, jotting down all those little verses and stuff—he should know how it is for an artist."

"I heard he's had some health issues. Maybe that's why he couldn't repay you?"

"That's news to me." Novelle's eyes narrowed. "Why are you so interested in Victor anyway?"

Sam forced a casual shrug. "Aside from needing some work done, I'm just thinking of his welfare. No one's seen him in a while. It's not like him to disappear without a word."

Novelle muttered, "Wouldn't surprise me if he skipped town to avoid his debts."

"Well, if you do hear from him," Sam said, rising from her seat, "let him know I'm looking for him, will you? For the repair work, I mean."

Novelle's gaze darted away, focusing intently on a spot on the far wall. The change was so sudden, it was as if Sam had flipped a switch.

"Well, you know Victor," Novelle said, her voice slightly higher than usual. "He probably just took off on some impromptu trip. He's always talking about visiting family in Mexico."

Sam nodded, but her instincts were on high alert. She'd known Victor for years, and spontaneous trips weren't his style. She'd *never* heard him talk about a visit to Mexico.

"Look," Novelle said, her voice tight, "I don't know where Victor is, okay? And frankly, I don't care. He owes me money, end of story."

Sam maintained her calm demeanor despite the artist's prickly response. She'd dealt with reluctant witnesses before, and pushing too hard now would not help.

"I understand," Sam said softly. "Debts can be a sensitive issue. I'm just trying to piece together what might have happened to him. Any information could help."

Novelle's jaw clenched. "Well, I can't help you. Now, if you'll excuse me, I have work to do."

With that, Novelle stood abruptly, gathering her sketchpad and pencils, wrapping her sandwich in a napkin and jamming it into her bag. She brushed past Sam without another word, elbowing her way through the crowd as she exited.

Sam sighed, deciding to keep the table and finish her lunch there. As she settled in with her tacos, her mind went back over the conversations of the morning. Novelle's defensiveness was telling, but what, exactly, it was telling her, Sam couldn't quite pin down.

Why so evasive about a simple debt? she wondered, taking a bite of crispy tortilla and chicken. Unless there was more to the story than just money. And Rosalita—what was her deal? Having power of attorney, telling people Victor was so ill he'd had to leave the country for treatment … Sam had heard of experimental medical procedures being done in Mexico. Could it be something like that?

Her phone buzzed as she was picking up the third taco. It was the bakery number.

"Sam, it's Jen. Um, we've had a slight mishap here and we'll need a two-by-four board."

"What … dare I ask?"

"Just call it a minor repair. Julio says he can fix it but needs the lumber."

"Okay then. The hardware store is on my way. Will thirty minutes be okay? I mean, no one's standing there propping up a broken table or something …"

"Nothing like that," Jen said with a laugh. "We'll see you in a half hour."

Sam set the phone down, puzzled, as she bit into her last taco. Ah. The window display. She'd used a cardboard box, covered in a tablecloth, to prop up one of the multi-tiered cakes in the display, and the temporary prop had most likely failed. Luckily, the display cakes were made of plastic, so there was probably no real damage, but it was nice of Julio to offer to construct a better base for it.

She sighed. At times like this she really missed Victor.

Chapter 7

Stepping out into the spring sunshine, Sam squinted against the brightness of the sky. She maneuvered her van out of the parking lot and headed toward the south end of town, where she could get a board for the bakery project.

The parking lot at Taos Hardware was crowded but she found a place near the garden center, locked the van, and walked into the building. The familiar scent of sawdust and newly cut lumber enveloped her, a comforting smell that reminded her of Beau's woodworking projects out in the barn. Narrow aisles stretched before her, cluttered with an eclectic array of tools, paint cans, and gardening supplies.

Sam's eyes scanned the store, her senses heightened. She could almost feel the residual energy of countless DIY dreams and home improvement projects that had started right here. As she navigated through the labyrinth of shelves, she heard a booming voice from the back of the store.

"I'm telling you, Joe, that new shipment of lumber is warped. It's gonna cause nothing but headaches."

Sam rounded the corner to find a tall, muscular man gesticulating wildly to the store owner, his long black braid swinging with each emphatic movement. She recognized Tommy Barker, a local contractor. Tommy had worked for Darryl Chartrain all through his high school years, becoming a good carpenter as he worked toward getting his contractor's license. She hung back, observing the interaction, hoping to get a chance to order her one board without a lot of drama.

"Look, Tommy," Joe replied, exasperation clear in his tone, "I can't control what comes in. Take it up with the supplier."

Tommy smirked. "Yeah, right. Like they'd listen to me." He was pointing a forefinger at the harried-looking store owner.

"Tommy," Sam said, injecting warmth into her voice. "It's good to see you again."

Tommy's head snapped around, his eyes narrowing as he registered Sam's presence. "Well, if it isn't Samantha Sweet," he drawled, leaning back against the sales counter. "What brings you to this neck of the woods? Baking supplies run out?"

Sam chuckled, unfazed by his brusque manner. "No, my mixing bowls are just fine, thanks. Actually, I just need a single two-by-four, and it doesn't even matter if it's warped."

Tommy, a little embarrassed at being overheard,

glanced at the store owner, who seemed relieved by the interruption. Joe met Sam's gaze and confirmed her order, then disappeared into the back room.

"Actually, Tommy, maybe you can answer something for me. Got a minute?"

"Yeah, sure," he grunted, turning to face Sam fully. "What's on your mind?"

Sam carefully considered her words. "I was wondering if you'd heard from Victor Martinez lately. It seems he's been scarce around town."

She watched Tommy's face closely, noting the slight tightening around his eyes and the way his jaw clenched at the mention of Victor's name.

"Martinez? Why would I keep tabs on that hack?"

"Now, Tommy …" Sam raised an eyebrow, her voice level. "I thought you two sometimes worked similar jobs. Professional courtesy and all that."

Tommy's laugh was sharp and humorless. "Courtesy? From the guy who tried to underbid me on every job?"

"So, you haven't seen him recently?" Sam interjected, steering the conversation back on track.

Tommy's eyes darted away for a split second before meeting hers again. "Nah, not for a while. Why? He in some kind of trouble?"

Sam shrugged, staying casual yet focused on Tommy's reactions. "Just seems to have dropped off the radar. Some of his regular customers are starting to worry."

"Well, that's real touching," Tommy sneered, "but I've got my own work to deal with. If Martinez can't handle his business, that's on him."

As Tommy spoke, Sam couldn't help but notice the slight tremor in his voice, the way his eyes wouldn't quite meet hers. There was more here than simple rivalry, she was certain of it.

Joe reappeared from the back, carrying a board. "Here you go, Ms. Sweet. One pine two-by-four. I chose one for you that's nice and straight."

Sam pulled out some cash and paid, thanking him, her tone light. "Have either of you heard anything about Victor Martinez being ill, going away for treatment?"

The question drew a blank look from Joe. "No, not at all. I haven't seen him around for a while, but that's pretty normal in the winter months."

Tommy winced. "That's a new one on me."

"Well, thanks for your time, Tommy. If either of you do happen to hear anything from Victor, would you let me know? I'd like to get in touch with him."

Tommy grunted noncommittally, already turning back to his argument with the store owner. "Yeah, sure, whatever. Now, about that lumber, Joe …"

As Sam turned away, her mind raced. Tommy's hostility toward Victor was evident, but was it enough to make the man a suspect in Victor's disappearance? Or was there something else lurking beneath the surface of Tommy's bravado?

"Ms. Sweet?" Tommy's face twisted into a smirk as he called after Sam. "You know, if you really want to know what happened to Victor, maybe you should be asking his wife."

Sam paused, walking back with a carefully neutral expression. "Rosalita? Why's that?"

Tommy leaned against the counter, his posture smug. "Let's just say she's got her fingers in all of Victor's pies now. Funny how she's suddenly managing his business, isn't it? And I hear she's even trying to sell his house."

Sam's eyebrows rose slightly. "Is that so? I hadn't heard about the house."

"Oh yeah," Tommy nodded, his voice dropping to a conspiratorial whisper. "That woman's always had dollar signs in her eyes. Wouldn't surprise me if she finally decided Victor wasn't worth as much to her alive as dead."

A chill ran down Sam's spine at the accusation. She kept her voice steady as she probed, "That's quite an allegation, Tommy. Do you have any proof?"

"Proof? I'm not a cop. But I've got eyes, and I've seen how she treated him. Always pushing, always wanting more. Victor frustrated the hell out of me, but he was basically a good guy, you know? Didn't deserve that kind of treatment."

As Tommy spoke, Sam's mind whirled. Could there be truth to his words? She'd known Rosalita slightly for years, but suddenly she felt as if she didn't know the woman at all.

"Well, thanks for the information," Sam said, her voice carefully neutral. "I appreciate you taking the time to talk." What did he mean when he referred to Victor as a competitor? She'd been under the impression Tommy was into new construction, not handyman jobs.

As she opened the back of her van and loaded the long board inside, Sam's mind churned. Tommy's accusations were serious, but his own history with Victor couldn't be ignored. And, she noticed, he had referred to Victor in the past tense.

Chapter 8

Back at Sweet's Sweets, Julio met Sam in the alley where she parked her van. He took the new board and already had tools ready to make the stand for the cake display. She noticed he'd borrowed from Victor's toolbox, and she felt a little pang. This was exactly the kind of small job she would have hired Victor to do, the indispensable task for her, a little extra income for him. While Julio set to work on the project, she went inside.

Becky was putting the finishing touches on a cake shaped like an Easter basket, complete with a fondant bunny and life-sized eggs decorated in pastels. Sam complimented her on the expert weave of the fondant 'wicker' and the details on the eggs.

"It's for Cassie Hurst at the daycare. They're doing an open house and one of the parents offered to pay for an over-the-top cake."

"The kids will absolutely love it." Sam set her bag down, slipped into her baker's jacket, and washed her hands while Becky went over the rest of the pending orders.

"One of these is for six dozen empanadas," Becky told her. "It's not due until Good Friday, but we might want to get a head start. Bessie Griego usually makes them for her big family gathering, but she broke her wrist last month and can't manage rolling out all that dough."

"She's one of the best cooks in town. No pressure there, for us."

"I'm sure we can come up with good ones. They want pineapple, cherry, and dulce de leche—two dozen of each."

"I've had Bessie's. I'll see if we can come close to duplicating the taste and texture of the dough she makes."

Becky set the basket cake aside. Sam pulled out two huge trays of sugar cookies Julio had baked in her absence and started whipping up a big batch of buttercream for them. Within fifteen minutes, she and Becky were piping decorations. At some point, Julio walked through with the sturdy base he'd created for the window display.

Sam held up sticky, icing-coated hands. "Jen can help you get that set up," she told him.

"Anything new in your investigation?" Becky asked, setting the first tray of completed cookies aside.

Sam told her about the two recent encounters, first with Novelle Rojas and later with Tommy Barker. "Tommy seems to think Rosalita is selling Victor's house. I was a little shocked at that. There was no signage out front when I went there. Short of going back and confronting Rosalita about it, I wonder how I can find out if it's true."

Becky pondered for a moment. "How about asking one of the real estate agents? Don't they all have access to a service that lists everything on the market?"

"Ah—brilliant!"

"Of course, Rosalita could be trying to sell it privately… but I'd bet the agents know. When my folks listed their house, a few years ago, they put up a For Sale by Owner sign and they got bombarded by Realtors right away."

Sam nodded. "Simpson Realty is right on the corner by the plaza. I've met the owner—she's a fanatic for our mocha brownies. I'll pop over there once the cookies are done." She glanced at the clock. It was a little after three. Plenty of time.

An hour later, she peered out the front window as she surveyed her front window display. Julio and Jen had done a brilliant job of reworking the setup, adding multiple levels on which to show off cakes and pastries that reflected the beauty of spring and the joy of the Easter season.

"I'm going to walk over to the plaza," she informed Jen, as she put two mocha brownies into one of their purple logo bags. The walk to the real estate office would help work out the kinks in her back, legs, and shoulders.

Her feet scuffed against the sidewalk as she approached the adobe building housing Talia Simpson's real estate office. The sky was a clear, deep blue, and Sam stretched her shoulders as she walked along with her little bakery bag. She pushed open the heavy wooden door, greeted by a cacophony of ringing phones and hurried voices.

The receptionist, a young woman with a cute, messy hairstyle had the phone receiver up to her ear. She quickly put the caller on hold and turned to Sam. "Welcome to Simpson Realty and Property Management. How can I help you?" She smiled politely toward Sam, but her eyes darted anxiously to the blinking phone lines.

"I'm here to see Talia Simpson," Sam said, keeping it quick. "Samantha Sweet. I don't have an appointment, but—" She held up the bakery bag with its treasure inside.

"Oh, Ms. Sweet, from the bakery!" The receptionist's eyes widened in recognition. "Of course. She's very busy today, but let me just see if she's available." She pressed a button on the phone console. "Ms. Simpson? Samantha Sweet is here to see you."

A pause. "It looks like she can see you now. Follow me."

As the young woman led the way down a wide corridor, Sam took in the office. Glossy photos of Taos properties lined the walls, the cerulean sky a constant backdrop. She could almost smell the sage and piñon through the images.

The receptionist knocked lightly on Talia's door before entering. She stood aside to let Sam walk inside.

The office was a study in controlled chaos. Stacks of papers teetered precariously on every surface, and a wall of filing cabinets loomed behind an oversized desk. Talia, a slender woman in her mid-sixties, looked as frazzled as her surroundings, her wild blonde hair seeming to crackle with nervous energy. She wore a mid-calf broomstick skirt, a velveteen tunic, and lots of turquoise jewelry. Her veined hands and weathered complexion spoke of way too much time in the sun.

"Sam! Come in, come in," Talia said, her smile a bit too wide to be genuine. She gestured to a chair across from her desk. "What can I do for you today?"

Sam placed the brownie bag on the desk and settled into the chair, her eyes never leaving Talia's face. "I'm curious whether a certain property is on the market." She gave Victor's address from memory.

"Well, let's just check that real quick. It's not one of

our listings, I do know that, but we can take a look at everything in the MLS." She tapped keys on her computer, clicked a couple of links, which Sam couldn't see. A tiny frown settled between her eyebrows. "Hm, I'm not finding that one."

"The owner is Victor Martinez. I'm not sure he's selling, but I heard a rumor."

Talia's smile faltered for a split second before reasserting itself. "Victor the landscape guy, the handyman?"

"You've worked with him? I guess I had heard that."

Talia's smile brightened. "Victor? Oh, yes, he's done odd jobs here and there. Why do you ask?"

"I'm trying to track him down," Sam said carefully. "No one seems to have seen him in a while."

"Oh, you know how he is. Probably off on one of his mysterious trips again. That man is as unreliable as they come."

It wasn't the first time someone had said Victor liked to travel, and Sam wondered why she was getting different stories about that. Among her own friends, it seemed the consensus that Victor was a homebody.

Sam's eyes locked on Talia's. "When was the last time you saw him, Talia?"

The realtor's gaze slid away, focusing on a point just over Sam's shoulder. "Oh, I couldn't say for certain. It's been quite busy here, you understand. Properties to show, deals to close …"

Way to change the subject. As Talia rambled on about her recent sales, Sam wondered. Why was Talia being so evasive? And what was that flicker of … something … she'd seen in the woman's eyes at the mention of Victor's name?

"Talia," Sam interrupted gently, "I know Victor did some repair work for you from time to time. Was there any problem with the job?"

Talia's smile became brittle. "Problem? No, no problem at all. Victor's work was … adequate. It's hard to hire good help here, and we had to take what we could get. Now, if you'll excuse me, Sam, I have a client coming in any minute."

Sam wanted to come back at her over that last comment. Victor had always done beautiful work for her. But she needed to keep this conversation pertinent, to gather information. "What about an illness? Did you have any idea he might have been sick, say, last fall or winter?"

Talia shrugged and shook her head.

Talia was hiding something, Sam felt sure. But what? Unlike the artist Novelle Rojas, this didn't seem to be about an unpaid debt.

Talia's polished nails drummed a staccato rhythm on her cluttered desk. "You know, if you really want to know about Victor Martinez, you should talk to that wife of his," she said, her voice taking on a sharp edge. "Rosalita's always meddling in his affairs, causing trouble."

Sam leaned forward, intrigued. Talia wasn't the first person to be under the impression that Victor and Rosalita were still married. "Trouble? How so?"

"Oh, she's been meddling in Victor's business affairs," Talia said. "Calling clients, canceling jobs, making excuses. It's cost me a number of delays and lost sales."

"Cancelling jobs?" This didn't align with what Rosalita had told her. "I thought Rosalita was managing Victor's work while he was … away."

Talia let out a harsh laugh. "Managing? Is that what

she's calling it? She wouldn't know the first thing about running a business. No, she's been sabotaging everything Victor built."

Then again, did Sam necessarily believe what the ex had said—not really. Something wasn't adding up, but she couldn't quite identify what made her think that.

"Thank you for your time, Talia," Sam said, rising from her chair. "You've been very … informative."

As she made her way through the bustling real estate office, she wondered if she was missing something crucial.

"Something's not adding up," she muttered to herself. "Novelle's accusations, Tommy's bitterness, Talia's defensiveness, and Rosalita's conflicting stories. I'm not sure who to believe, at this point."

Out on the street again, a group of tourists passed by, their chatter a stark contrast to Sam's reflective mood. She nodded politely, maintaining her small-town friendliness even as she felt preoccupied.

She paused at the corner of Kit Carson Road, her gaze drawn to the nearby mountains as she waited for the light to change. The snowy top of Wheeler Peak was a reminder that no matter how uncertain life became, some things were constant.

The traffic stopped and she crossed the plaza, her thoughts swirling randomly until the familiar sight of Sweet's Sweets came into view, its cheerful exterior with its purple awning brightening her mood once again.

Inside, the late-afternoon rush was in full swing and Sam quickly switched to customer service mode. Jen was handing out cookies to kids, while their mothers grabbed a cup of coffee and slice of cheesecake. Sam waited on two people who had come to pick up special-order cakes, boxing them and running their credit card tickets.

And gradually, the jumble of conversations from earlier in the day receded as Sam shut down the kitchen and walked out back to her van at six o'clock.

Ten minutes later, she pulled into the driveway at home, the late afternoon sun casting long shadows across the pasture beyond the barn. As she climbed out of the van, their Lab and border collie raced to greet her.

"Hey, Ranger. Hey, Nellie," she greeted, reaching down to rub their ears and absorb some of their boundless optimism. Dogs really are the best, she decided as she unlocked the front door.

Beau's truck was parked in its usual spot, but Sam realized he was probably using his department cruiser when she called out a greeting to an empty house. She wandered into the kitchen to figure out something for dinner, settling on leftover green chile stew. Tomorrow she really needed to get to the market for fresh produce.

The sound of Beau's vehicle caught the dogs' attention, just about the time the stew began to simmer.

"Hey, darlin' how's it going?" he asked as soon as he walked inside.

He hung up his jacket and joined her in the kitchen, greeting her with a kiss that still had the power to make her heart flutter.

"Did you have a good day?" he asked.

"I've talked to a lot of people about Victor Martinez. More questions than answers, at this point." She reached for soup bowls while he washed up.

"Yeah, tell me about it. Things in the office were crazy today." He carried the basket of warm tortillas to the table as she set the steaming bowls down. "That meeting in Santa

Fe the other day has upended my whole job description."

Sam put aside all the questions she'd meant to ask him about Victor's situation. Once they settled at the table, Beau was full of news about the latest from the state legislature, a whole raft of new rules and paperwork they were now requiring from every division of law enforcement in the county.

She put on her best wifely smile and listened attentively. Clearly, since her investigation consisted of way more questions than answers, it would have to wait for another conversation.

Chapter 9

Sam cruised slowly past Victor's adobe house, its earth-toned walls stark against the deep blue Taos sky. She'd awakened this morning with a curiosity about whether the rumor was true about the house going up for sale and someone's comment that Rosalita might have simply put up a For Sale by Owner sign. But there was no evidence of that—yet.

The same beat-up white Nissan was parked at an odd angle in the driveway, as if Rosalita had been in a hurry. So, okay, Sam had a lot more questions and there was no time like the present. And she had handled the wooden box this morning, hoping to draw more energy for her bakery work, but there could be an added benefit to talking with her chief suspect right now, too. She pulled over to the curb, two houses away.

The conversation with Beau over breakfast lingered in her mind. "Be careful, honey," he had said, his ocean blue eyes serious beside the salt-and-pepper hair at his temples. "Word has it that Rosalita's got a temper, and if she's up to something …"

Sam approached the front door, the gravel crunching beneath her feet.

Knock, knock, knock. The sound echoed in the still morning air. Sam waited, straining to hear any movement inside. Nothing. She tried the handle, finding it unyielding.

"Rosalita?" she called out, peering through the window. The curtains were drawn tight, blocking any view of the interior.

Frustrated, Sam pressed her palm against the cool glass, closing her eyes. Sometimes, if she concentrated hard enough, she could sense … something. An impression, a lingering energy. But today, there was nothing but an eerie stillness.

"Where are you, Victor?" she whispered, irritation bubbling up within her. "And what on earth is Rosalita up to?"

She stepped back, surveying the property once more. Obviously, Rosalita wasn't tending the yard. As on her previous visit here, Victor's usually immaculate garden looked neglected, weeds sprouting in the normally tended beds.

Ideas buzzed through her head, piecing together the puzzle. Rosalita's ever-changing stories, Victor's sudden disappearance, the power of attorney … None of it added up to anything good.

"I'm not leaving until I get some answers," Sam declared, wondering if Victor's ex was standing inside, listening. She settled in to wait, determined to uncover the truth hidden behind those closely drawn curtains.

A faint scraping sound from the side of the house caught Sam's attention. Her heart quickened as she stepped off the porch. She moved cautiously around the perimeter, every sense on high alert.

As she rounded the corner, Sam paused. There, emerging from a tool shed, was Rosalita. The older woman's shape filled the doorway, her dyed black hair gleaming in the morning sun.

Play it cool, Sam. See what you can learn.

With a casual wave, Sam called out, "Morning, Rosalita! Didn't expect to see you here."

Rosalita's head snapped up, her eyes widening momentarily before a forced smile spread across her face. "Oh, Señora Sweet! What a surprise," she replied, her voice overly cheerful. She wiped her hands nervously on a towel, leaving faint smudges of … was that dirt?

Sam's gaze flicked between Rosalita's face and her hands. What have you been up to? she wondered silently.

"I was just delivering a cake in the neighborhood," Sam lied smoothly, walking across the back yard toward her. "Thought I'd drop by and see if you've heard anything about when Victor might be coming back."

Rosalita's smile faltered for a split second. "Ah, no, I'm afraid not. He's still doing his treatments."

Sam nodded sympathetically, all the while noting how Rosalita's eyes darted around, never quite meeting her gaze. The woman's smile tightened. "That's too bad," Sam replied, her tone light despite the suspicion churning in her gut. "I hope he feels better soon. Victor's always been so dedicated to his garden. It must be hard for you to see it looking a bit … neglected."

Rosalita's expression hardened almost imperceptibly. "Yes, well, I have been doing my best to keep up with things. It is a lot of work, you know."

Remembering Beau's warning, Sam wondered—was she facing a cornered animal, unpredictable and potentially dangerous?

Sam nodded. "Have you spoken to Victor recently?" she asked, her tone casual. "Several people have asked me if he'll be back to work on their properties."

Rosalita's grip tightened on the towel, her knuckles whitening. "Of course," she replied, a touch too quickly. "We spoke just last night, in fact. He's doing as well as can be expected, considering his condition."

Sam raised an eyebrow.

Rosalita shrugged. "Nothing serious, you understand. But he's asked me to manage things while he's away. His affairs, the business, all of it."

Something wasn't adding up. 'Nothing serious' didn't exactly fit with his being under medical treatment for months on end.

"So you're handling the landscaping business? That's quite a responsibility. How's it holding up without him?"

Rosalita's smile tightened. "Oh, you know how it is with small businesses. Ups and downs. But I assure you, everything's under control. I have hired some young workers, his nephew Marcos, for one."

"That's good!" Sam smiled, as if she believed it. "So, may I tell his customers they can call you to set up appointments?"

"Oh, well … it's a small crew and we're fully booked for the whole month already."

"And do you expect Victor to come back by then?"

Rosalita's smile faltered, her eyes darting to the unkempt garden behind Sam. "It depends on his recovery," she said, her tone dismissive. "He needs time and space to heal. I'm sure you understand."

The conversation felt like it was going in circles and then being shut down, like a door slamming in her face. But she wasn't ready to let go just yet.

"Of course, I understand," she replied, nodding sympathetically. "It must be challenging, managing everything in Victor's absence," she said, her voice casual. "Especially with all the legal aspects. Someone said you're selling his house—using your power of attorney, I presume?"

The words hung in the air between them. Sam watched Rosalita carefully, noting how her eyes widened slightly at the mention of legalities. It was a subtle reaction, but to Sam's trained eye, it spoke volumes.

"I … yes, of course," Rosalita stammered, recovering quickly. "Victor trusts me completely with his affairs. Now, if you'll excuse me, I have many tasks to attend to."

Sam grasped for a topic that would get her inside the house to check things out, see if she spotted evidence of where Victor was. "I heard you're selling some furniture. Could you show me?"

"I've been organizing and cleaning everything. It's a big task, you know."

Sam could almost see the gears turning in Rosalita's head, desperately searching for a distraction as she led the way back toward the front yard. She followed Rosalita toward the house, wanting to ask where Victor would live if his house was sold, but she was sure Rosalita would have a quick answer for that, too.

As they walked, Sam's eyes darted around, taking in details about the property. Two shovels and a hoe, along with several smaller implements, lay scattered haphazardly across the yard, looking more like abandoned evidence than gardening equipment. A riding mower covered in winter grime was parked next to the shed.

A faint, earthy scent caught Sam's attention. It was the unmistakable smell of freshly turned soil, incongruous with the neglected state of the garden. Why would anyone be digging in a garden they clearly weren't maintaining?

"Watch your step," Rosalita called over her shoulder, navigating around a cluster of upturned flowerpots.

Sam carefully sidestepped the obstacles as they circled the house, unable to shake the edgy feeling that had settled over her. Thinking of Beau's warning, she picked up a sharp-edged hand shovel, pretending to examine it. She slipped it into the deep pocket of her jacket when the other woman wasn't looking.

Rosalita unlocked and pushed open the front door, revealing a dim interior cluttered with cardboard boxes and miscellaneous items. Sam blinked, adjusting to the low light as she stepped inside.

Rosalita gestured vaguely toward a stack of boxes near the wall. "These are some things Victor wanted to get rid of. Mostly junk, if you ask me."

Sam nodded, feigning interest as her eyes scanned the room. Amidst the clutter, a small statue on an end table caught her attention. Its intricate design seemed oddly out of place among the mundane objects surrounding it.

"That's an interesting piece," Sam commented, moving closer to the statue. "Mind if I take a look?"

Rosalita's eyes narrowed, a flicker of hesitation crossing her face. "Oh, that old thing? It's nothing special, really."

Why was Rosalita so reluctant? "I'd still love to see it, if you don't mind," Sam pressed gently.

After a moment's pause, Rosalita relented with a forced smile. "All right, go ahead. It's Saint Fiacre, the patron saint of gardeners. Victor was fond of it."

Sam carefully lifted the statue, but she could feel Rosalita's eyes boring into her. The woman's sudden intensity was palpable, setting Sam's nerves on edge.

Why is she so intent on this statue? Sam wondered, turning the piece over in her hands. What secrets could it possibly hold?

Sam touched the intricate details of the statue, subtly tapping to see if it seemed hollow. It didn't. "It's beautifully crafted," she remarked, keeping her tone casual. "Did Victor commission it?"

Rosalita shrugged, her gaze never leaving Sam's hands. "Some local artist made it. I think they gave it to him."

Sam turned the statue over, and a small mark on the bottom caught her eye. Her heart skipped a beat as she recognized the signature: N.R.

Novelle Rojas. She carefully smoothed her expression.

"Interesting," Sam murmured, setting the statue back down. "Victor certainly had an eye for unique pieces."

Rosalita nodded curtly, clearly eager to move on. "Yes, well, he always did have strange tastes."

Novelle claimed that Victor owed her money, so why would she give away what was obviously a quality—probably valuable—piece? This new connection between Novelle and Victor was unexpected and potentially significant. Maybe she assumed he would pay for the statue, and that was the source of her anger. But no, the artist had specifically told Sam she had loaned him cash.

Sam scanned the space, noting a doorway to a kitchen and a hallway that probably led to bedrooms. But Rosalita didn't pick up the hint; she'd, in fact, planted herself deliberately to block the hall.

"Thank you for showing me around, Rosalita," Sam said, injecting warmth into her voice. "I appreciate your taking the time."

Rosalita not-so-subtly herded her toward the door, and Sam really had a feeling that the woman was hiding something crucial—her body language, her eyes darting nervously.

"It's no trouble," Rosalita replied with an insincere smile. "I'm sure Victor would want his friends to check in."

Sam nodded, mentally already jumping ahead to her next steps. She needed to get back inside that house when the other woman wasn't around. "Take care, Rosalita. Tell Victor we hope he comes home soon."

As Sam made her way back to her van, she slipped the small shovel out of her pocket and tossed it on the ground behind a bush, thankful she hadn't felt the need for a weapon. Still, the implications of what she'd discovered swirled in her mind. The statue, Novelle's involvement, the patch of turned earth in the back yard, Rosalita's strange behavior—it all pointed to a deeper mystery than she'd initially suspected.

What's the connection here? And what is Rosalita really hiding?

The van hummed along the quiet street, and Sam couldn't get rid of the image of Rosalita's nervous eyes, the way she'd tried to deflect attention from the statue.

"It just feels like ... there's something about that statue

that Rosalita doesn't want me to know."

She pulled over to the side of the road, fishing her phone out of her pocket. After a moment's hesitation, she dialed a familiar number.

"Beau? It's me. I think I've stumbled onto something that could be important."

Her husband's deep voice crackled through the speaker. "What's going on, Sam? You all right?"

"I'm fine," she assured him. "But I need you to run a check on a Novelle Rojas. She claims Victor owes her money, but Rosalita tells me she gave Victor a pretty valuable statue."

"Novelle?" Beau sounded surprised. "The artist? And you're thinking …"

Sam sighed. "I'm not sure yet. Just wondering if Novelle tried to pursue the debt through legal channels. Or maybe claimed the statue was stolen?"

There was a pause on the other end of the line. "All right, I'll see what we can dig up. I'm kind of swamped, so I'll put Rico on the search for court cases and all that. And Sam, be careful. If there's something shady going on …"

"I know, I know," Sam said, a small smile playing on her lips despite the tension. "I'll leave the dangerous stuff to you, Sheriff. For now, I'm just connecting dots."

They ended the call when Beau's office intercom buzzed him.

"Time to pay a visit to our local art scene," Sam decided, pulling back onto the road.

Chapter 10

Sam parked in the municipal lot behind the Bent Street shops, stuck a few quarters in the meter, and walked along the shady walkway to La Galleria. According to her quick research foray on Google, this was the local shop that featured Novelle Rojas's work.

She had two goals: Find out the value of the little *santo* she'd seen in Victor's house. And, if she was lucky enough to get a gossipy person to talk to, learn whether Novelle was actually earning a living with her art. Not to be judgmental, but it would help explain how far the artist might go to punish Victor for an unpaid two-hundred-dollar debt. Plus, Sam was really curious.

The front windows of the gallery displayed large canvases depicting Taos life, street scenes in vivid hues, each painting done in a completely different style. The one on the left reminded her of the artist Betty Sabo, whose realistic depictions of snow on adobe dwellings could take your breath away. The other, to the right of the entrance, showed the distinctive style of Amado Peña, the Pascua Yaqui artist so well known throughout the Southwest. This one showed a seated man in a large hat, a brightly colored serape over one shoulder. Sam paused to admire them for a full minute before walking inside.

Her attention to the art had drawn notice, and a young man in a thousand-dollar suit and two-hundred-dollar haircut greeted her. His professional cool vanished when he recognized her.

"Oh my gosh, you're the cookie lady!"

Sam laughed. "I suppose I am. But I'm afraid I don't remember your name."

"Artie Beacon. I know—Artie who works in an *art* gallery. You don't need to say it—all my friends tease me constantly. My mom used to take me to your bakery every Friday afternoon for a cookie after school."

They shared a little memory-moment. Artie had grown up, gotten a fine arts degree, and settled into what was a dream job for him.

Sam got right to the point. "I'm interested in sculptures by Novelle Rojas. I saw one at a friend's house."

"Ah, Novelle." He might have tried to hide his infatuation with the artist, but he didn't succeed. And even though she was probably nearly a decade his senior, well, hope springs eternal, Sam supposed. He led the way to a cozy alcove where several *santos* stood in their own niches.

"St. Joseph, the patron saint of fatherhood, is also a favorite among the real estate crowd," he said, pointing to each sculpture in turn. "Of course, St. Christopher for the travelers among us, and St. Francis of Assisi celebrates nature and living in harmony." He stood back and let Sam examine them.

"They're beautiful. May I hold one?"

"Only because I know you have a very delicate touch with pastry," he joked, handing her the St. Joseph.

She turned it over. The signature marking on the bottom was identical to the one on St. Fiacre at Victor's house.

"And the price? Assuming it's not in the range of 'if you have to ask, you can't afford it'?"

Artie laughed again. "Well, not quite that high. These range from two thousand to twenty-five hundred."

Sam gulped and handed it back to him. "I'm sure they are absolutely worth that, but it's a little out of my range." And she would bet out of Victor's range, as well. "Do you sell a lot of them?"

He nodded, checking to be sure no one else was nearby. "Quite a few."

"Novelle must be making a pretty decent living …?"

"It would be inappropriate for me to speculate about that." He was nodding as he said it. "Keep in mind that she also works in pastels and collage, in addition to her sculptures, and her work is sold in Santa Fe, Dallas, and New York. I can show you a few …"

Sam followed him across the room, thinking all the while that there was no way to describe Novelle Rojas as a starving artist. And she certainly didn't have a motive for harming Victor Martinez over a two-hundred-dollar loan he never repaid.

Still, it was curious why she'd made such a fuss over it the day Sam met her. Maybe she was just one of those people who always paid her own debts and expected everyone else to act exactly the same.

After a half hour, Sam purchased some pretty notecards and assured Artie he could still come by Sweet's Sweets any time. If he asked for her, she'd see to it that he got his favorite cookie.

Well, that trip seemed to eliminate one suspect in Victor's disappearance, Sam thought as she unlocked her van, or at least the obvious motive. There were still a few minutes left on her parking meter, so she sat there in the shade and phoned the bakery. Jen told her everything was going well. Becky would have some deliveries ready to go by early afternoon, but for the moment, Sam didn't need to be there.

One more call, this time asking for Deputy Rico at the sheriff's office.

"I was just about to call you, Sam," he said. "About Novelle Rojas—I didn't find anything at all in the court records about her pursing Victor Martinez for an unpaid debt. Sorry."

"That's okay. I appreciate the effort. I have one other favor. Victor's nephew is a young guy named Marcos Sanchez. I want to chat with him but don't have any contact details. Can you …?"

"Sure. But don't tell Beau I'm doing this. We're not supposed to be able to spy on private citizens."

"Spy?"

"Well, track them through their vehicle records and such."

Ten minutes later, she had an address and was steering her van toward it. The route took her down a couple of side streets, to an area where warehouses had cropped up between older, cheaper apartment buildings. A trucking company sat to the north and an automotive repair shop to the south of the apartment she was looking for. The building had probably been there since the early '70s. It was of that style, with five units on the ground floor and five above, served by rusted metal stairways at either end of the building. It wasn't the kind of place with amenities.

Two cars sat in the lot in front of the building, both of them basic little sedans, both at least fifteen years old. And then there was one fairly new, shiny black pickup truck, tricked out with all the chrome bumpers and extra light bars you could possibly put on it. Sam would bet money that the vehicle cost more than the entire building had, back when it was built.

She pulled her bakery van to the far end of the lot, consulting the note she'd made, finding the apartment on the ground level, in the middle of the row. The shiny black truck was parked directly in front of it. It seemed evident that Marcos Sanchez valued fancy wheels more than luxury living. She wondered if Uncle Victor was subsidizing him.

She slung her bag over her shoulder and walked toward unit 103. She was nearly there when she realized the screen door was closed but the wooden door behind it stood open. From inside she heard the clatter of an aluminum can skittering across the floor and hitting something with a loud rattle. Sam paused, remaining to one side.

"Stubborn old man," a male voice growled, seemingly to himself, as there was no response. "I just needed a little help, *Tio*, just to get caught up on bills." Then the voice took on a mocking tone. " '*Lo siento, sobrino.* I can't keep bailing you out.' Well, screw that."

Sam cleared her throat and tapped on the screen door. "Hello? Anyone home?"

The muttering immediately stopped and a young man stepped into view. "Yeah?"

"Marcos Sanchez?"

"Who wants to know?"

"I'm a friend of Victor Martinez, and I was talking to Rosalita yesterday ... I understand you're Victor's nephew."

His brows pulled together and he stepped closer to the screen. She took in his baggy clothing, chocolate-colored eyes, dark hair, cut in a style she'd seen a lot of teens wearing. His age might be anywhere between fifteen and twenty-five, but she guessed he was probably in his late teens, based on things she'd heard about him.

"Nice truck." Sam tilted her head toward the pickup and watched a smile creep over his face.

"Yeah. Love that thing."

"Look, I've been a little worried about Victor. A lot of us usually hire him to keep our gardens in shape, and we haven't heard from him."

He shrugged, in a so-what manner.

"Have you? Heard from him in recent weeks?"

His eyes rolled impatiently, clearly not interested in answering questions for some old lady who knew his uncle.

"Look, I'm just trying to gather information, to help Victor out if there's some problem ... but I can turn it over to the sheriff if necessary. Do you have a few minutes to talk?"

Whether it was her persistence or the mention of the sheriff, something in Marcos relented and he pushed the screen open. "You might as well come in."

Sam stepped into a living room that had been decorated by a tornado. Marcos scooped up an armful of shirts and jeans from the battered faux-leather sofa and tossed them through a doorway, presumably into the bedroom. An old boombox sat on an end table, nearly covered with magazines and papers. The beer can she'd heard from outside lay against the baseboard under the front window, and several others sat on the floor around a saggy recliner chair.

"I'm having a beer," he said, heading toward the refrigerator that anchored the tiny kitchen, which consisted of a two-burner stove, a narrow sink, and about six inches of counter space. "You want one?"

Sam held up a hand, wondering if he was older than he looked, or if someone else was supplying the beer. "I'm fine, thanks."

He popped the top on the Tecate and perched on the edge of the recliner. "So, Tio Victor … what's the problem? You gotta understand, I don't see him much."

"Do you remember the last time you did see him?"

"Yeah." He took a long swig. "Him and me, we kinda got into it outside Taos Hardware. Alls I did was ask for a little loan. My truck payment was due the next week. Rent, the week after that. And there's some credit card bills … you know, for dates and hanging with the guys."

"And he turned you down."

"What does he know anyway?" Marcos grumbled, kicking aside a stack of mail in which Sam spotted some overdue notices. "Old man can barely speak English."

He slumped into the sagging recliner, springs creaking in protest. He took another long pull on the beer. "Easy for him to say," he growled. "He's got that witch Rosalita managing everything now."

Sam's interest picked up. She let him talk.

He began mimicking, his voice dripping with false

sweetness: "'Oh, Marcos, dear. I'm afraid Victor's affairs are no longer any of your business. I have power of attorney now.' Power of attorney," Marcos spat, standing up abruptly. "More like she's got her claws in everything. This woman came into his life right after Tia Maria died, caught him at a ... what do you say..."

"A vulnerable time?"

"Yeah. They fought a lot and got a divorce. They weren't even married five years. I don't know why she's still around." He paced the small room, his anger building. "She's probably bleeding him dry, and he's too blind to see it. And now she's got control of the business too? This isn't right."

"Yeah, Rosalita said she was running the business. She told me she'd hired you and some other guys to do the work and keep it going."

"That's the first I'm hearing of it. She's bullshitting you."

Sam filed that away for later, two versions of the same story.

He paced back to the kitchen area and tossed his empty beer can in the sink. "There's got to be a way to expose her," he muttered. "I'll show Tio Victor what she really is. I should just go over there and demand the loan from *her*," he muttered, his voice lacking its previous force. "But that conniving *bruja* would probably just laugh in my face."

"You could be right about that," Sam agreed. Her gaze settled on a photo of the black pickup truck. It held a place of honor next to a flat-screen TV.

"I swore I'd pay him back. And then he says, 'You need to learn to manage your money.' He didn't understand! I told him, times are tough, man. How am I supposed to get ahead? And then I just got a lecture. I didn't need that."

Marcos's phone buzzed, jolting him back to the present. He glanced at the screen, his mouth twisting in a grimace. "Big Jay wants to go out for beers tonight."

He caught Sam's skeptical expression.

"*Mierda*," he muttered, tossing the phone aside. "Can't even afford a night out anymore."

Staring toward the water-stained ceiling, Marcos's bravado suddenly deflated. "I'll figure something out," he said, but his voice lacked conviction. His cocky façade crumbled a little as he grudgingly admitted to himself, "Maybe Tio Victor had a point. I've been throwing money around like some big shot, and now look at me."

The realization stung, clashing with his previous demeanor. He muttered, "But damn, did he have to be so stubborn about it? A small loan wouldn't have killed him. Maybe Tio Victor was right, after all. But how the hell do I fix this mess now?"

"Marcos … if I may …? I've been there. I rebelled at a young age, left home, a kid set on making it on my own, and I ended up with a child to support. Before that happens to you, I'd suggest you find a way to earn money that doesn't involve asking your relatives for it—and keep it legal. Trade school, night classes, or something. Right now, your expenses aren't that high." She glanced out the window at the shiny truck. "Well, some of them are. Trim back if you can and start looking for a real job." She stood. "And that's all I have in the way of advice."

She pulled a pen from her bag and scribbled her phone number on one of the envelopes laying in the mail stack. "If you do hear anything from Victor, please, let me know." And then she got out of there before he accused her of being just another old lady delivering a lecture.

Chapter 11

Okay, so who's on my list now, Sam mused as she stopped by Sweet's Sweets to pick up the orders for delivery. Novelle Rojas had some anger toward Victor, but didn't seem likely as a killer. Rosalita … who knew? With access to Victor's house, and if she truly did have power of attorney, she was better off to keep Victor alive but out of the way. That house had surely appreciated by a bunch, especially since the Hollywood crowd began increasingly moving into the area and buying up prime real estate. Could she have purposely made him sick so he would leave?

And then there was Marcos. Anger aplenty, a real sense of entitlement. And the kid was so mixed up. On the one hand, he thought Victor should simply finance his whims. On the other, he seemed to understand that he needed to grow up and take charge of his own life. Sam wouldn't place any trust in that one, not knowing what kind of temper he might be hiding.

She loaded a three-tier anniversary cake into the van, secured it, and went back in for an elaborate birthday cake—a further reminder of the whims of the rich. This was a five-tier concoction of circus animals and magical creatures, for a baby just turning a year old. She started the van and headed toward the birthday party first.

The huge house existed on a lot that had originally been the site of a home about the same size as Victor's, with a couple acres surrounding it. But the billionaire tech mogul who bought the property had razed the original place and erected a mansion that was an insult to the traditional style of the area. Sam realized, when she pulled into the long driveway, that this was only two blocks over from Victor's house. It gave her the perfect excuse to cruise past and see if anything had changed.

She handed off the birthday cake to a maid and left. Driving past Victor's humble home, she immediately saw that Rosalita's car was in the driveway again. She turned around in a neighboring driveway, hoping the woman hadn't seen her distinctive van with its paint job of enticing pastries.

After the anniversary cake had been safely delivered to the customer on the north end of town, Sam decided to make one more pass by Victor's place on her way back to the bakery. The fact that someone had been digging in the backyard had been nagging at her and she couldn't let go of the idea Rosalita had been up to something unsavory.

This time, she swung by home and swapped the van for her less-conspicuous personal truck. Fifteen minutes later, she was parked under a willow tree a half block away, her gaze fixed on the weathered adobe house down the block. The afternoon sun cast long shadows across the quiet Taos street. As Rosalita's distinctive figure emerged from the front door, Sam's pulse quickened.

"About time," she muttered, watching the older woman climb into her car and drive off in the opposite direction.

Sam pulled the carved wooden box from her bag and held it on her lap, its familiar warmth spreading through her fingertips. A flash of Victor's face flickered in her mind, gone as quickly as it appeared. She stashed the box safely beneath the truck seat.

Stepping out to the street, Sam paused to survey the neighborhood. The silence was almost eerie, broken only by the distant bark of a dog. As she approached Victor's house, her footsteps seemed unnaturally loud.

"You've done this before, Sam," she reminded herself, recalling her days as a USDA caretaker. "Just not for personal reasons."

At the front door, Sam hesitated. What if she was wrong? What if Victor really was in Mexico? But Rosalita's contradictory stories nagged at her. She needed to verify this.

"No turning back now," Sam muttered, raising her hand to knock.

The sound echoed through the house, seeming to mock her with its hollowness. Sam waited, straining to hear any movement inside. Nothing. She knocked again, harder this time.

"Victor?" she called out, going through the motions but knowing it was futile. "It's Samantha Sweet. Are you there?"

Silence answered her, reaffirming what she already

suspected. Victor wasn't here, and hadn't been for some time. But where was he? And why was Rosalita lying?

Sam thought of Beau, her sheriff husband, and what he'd say if he knew what she was up to. But, he'd said this wasn't a case for law enforcement—not yet, anyway.

"I'm sorry, Victor," she whispered, touching the doorknob. "But I need to know what happened to you."

With a final glance over her shoulder, Sam reached into her pocket, finding the familiar shapes of her lock picks, a remnant from her days of breaking into abandoned houses. She never thought she'd use these skills again, but here she was.

Sam easily inserted the tension wrench and pick into the lock. Her hands moved swiftly, feeling for the pins. Within moments, she heard the satisfying click.

"Still got it," she murmured, a tiny bit of pride in her voice.

The door creaked open, and Sam stepped inside, immediately enveloped by the stillness of the house. It felt even more abandoned than before, frozen in time. Her senses, heightened by adrenaline and the effects of touching the wooden box, picked up on the stagnant air.

Rosalita's been busy in the kitchen, Sam thought, catching a whiff of cumin and chili. The faint scent hung in the air.

She moved cautiously through the entryway, her eyes darting from corner to corner. The packing boxes were gone now, the overall effect neater, less cluttered. Everything looked normal, yet it still felt off. A framed photo of Victor and Rosalita caught her attention. Victor's kind eyes seemed to follow her, almost pleading. She wondered if he had kept the memento or if Rosalita had set it in place.

"Where are you, Victor?" Sam whispered. "What happened here?"

Her gaze swept the room, searching for anything out of place. The stack of unopened mail she'd seen during her previous visit, on a side table, was gone now. A thin layer of dust covered the kiva fireplace. Small details that spoke volumes.

The sculpture of St. Fiacre, probably the most valuable item in the house, was gone.

Sam took a deep breath. The place surely held clues, and she needed to find them. She moved swiftly through the living room, her footsteps muffled on the worn carpet, and into the hall. In the main bedroom, she paused, taking in the scene. The bed was meticulously made, hospital corners crisp and tight. Rosalita's work, Sam thought, remembering the housekeeper's reputation for fastidiousness. Her eyes narrowed as she scanned the room.

"No men's shoes or clothing," she murmured, peering into the closet. "No cologne on the dresser. Victor's presence has been … erased."

The bathroom yielded similar results. No toothbrush in the holder. Floral-scented toiletries dominated the counter.

"If Victor went to Mexico, he took everything with him," Sam reasoned. "But who packs their entire life for a temporary trip, especially when they're ill? More likely, Rosalita packed up his things."

She began a methodical search, deftly rifling through drawers and probing shelves. Years of experience as a USDA caretaker had honed her skills, making her movements quick and efficient.

"Come on, Victor," she whispered. "Give me something to work with."

Her hand brushed against a stack of papers in the bottom drawer of the nightstand. Heart quickening, she pulled them out, hope rising.

"Bills, grocery lists, a recipe for chile rellenos," Sam muttered, disappointment in her voice as she sifted through the mundane documents. "Nothing out of the ordinary."

Her frustration mounted. "What am I missing? There has to be more to this story than I'm seeing here."

Sam moved into the kitchen, her eyes sweeping over the neat countertops and gleaming appliances. As she scanned the room, a flash of color caught her eye, a cookbook, partially hidden behind a row of spice jars, yet beckoning to her somehow.

"Well, hello there," she murmured, reaching for the book. As she touched the worn cover, a familiar warm sensation caressed her arm. Sam inhaled sharply, recognizing the pull of magic from the carved wooden box she'd handled a few minutes ago.

"What secrets are you hiding?" she whispered, carefully opening the cookbook. The pages seemed to hum with energy, and Sam felt a vision forming in her mind—flashes of symbols and whispered incantations mingling with the recipes. She remembered Victor telling her once that his grandmother had been a *curandera*, a healer.

Excited, Sam began to flip through the pages. "This is more than just a collection of recipes," she thought, marveling at the intricate designs jotted in the margins. "Victor, how cool that you kept this old book."

Two small slips of paper fell from between the pages, fluttering to the floor like fallen leaves. Sam bent to retrieve them. One was a receipt of some kind and she dropped it into her bag after a quick glance. The other was on notepaper. Eagerly, she unfolded the note, instantly recognizing Victor's distinct handwriting.

"Okay …" she breathed, "what have you left behind, my friend?"

Samantha's eyes widened as she read the words scrawled on the note: *Ella se lo llevará todo a menos que la detenga.* She stumbled over the Spanish: "Something about 'she will take' …" But she couldn't decipher the rest of it. She found herself reading the cryptic message again.

"Who is 'she'?" Sam muttered, studying the hurried penmanship. "And something to stop?"

Well, the main 'she' in Victor's life was certainly Rosalita. Sam glanced around the kitchen, suddenly feeling exposed. The stale air seemed to press in on her, and she could almost hear Beau's voice in her head, cautioning her to be careful. But the pull of the mystery was too strong to ignore. "Why would he leave such an incriminating note where his ex might find it?"

"I need to be sure I'm understanding this correctly," she decided. "Rico's Spanish is way better than mine. I'll stop by and have him give me the translation."

She tucked the paper carefully into her pocket. "Maybe it's about Novelle Rojas," she mused, recalling the sculptor's claims of unpaid debts. "Or … I suppose there might be someone else in Victor's life we don't know about."

"Oh, Victor," she sighed, her voice barely above a whisper in the empty kitchen. "What mess have you gotten yourself into?"

She straightened her shoulders. "I'm going to get to the bottom of this," she vowed, patting her pocket where the note rested. "Whatever it takes, I'll uncover the truth behind your words, my friend. And I pray it's not too late to help you."

Samantha's keen eyes walked through the kitchen once again, touching the cool Mexican tile countertops as she moved methodically from one cabinet to the next. She pulled open a drawer, the flatware inside neatly organized, betraying no secrets.

"Nothing out of the ordinary here," she murmured, closing it softly. "But there's got to be something more."

She hesitated over the handle of a lower cabinet, but she reminded herself of the importance of thoroughness.

"You never know where the clues might be hiding," Sam whispered to herself, crouching down to peer into the dark recesses of the cabinet.

As she rummaged through pots and pans, a nagging thought tugged at her conscience. "What would Beau think if he knew I was here?" She imagined her husband's sternest sheriff-face. "He'd probably tell me I'm crossing a line. But sometimes, you have to bend the rules to find the truth."

Finding nothing of interest in the kitchen, Sam's attention turned to the small desk tucked in the corner of the living room. Victor's workspace was perfectly neat, as if someone had recently tidied it—Rosalita, no doubt. Sam thought of the boxes Rosalita said were things Victor wanted her to dispose of. She spotted a stack of papers in the top drawer, the handwriting distinctly feminine.

"Rosalita's been busy," Sam observed, as she examined a checkbook filled with recent entries. "Looks like she really has taken over the finances, as she told me."

She picked up another photo of Victor, noticing the empty spaces on the desk where other personal items should have been. "It does look like he left in a hurry," she mused aloud. "But did he go willingly, or was he forced out?"

Numerous questions filled her head as she contemplated the implications. "If Rosalita's managing everything, does that mean Victor's really gone for good? Or is she simply taking advantage of his absence?"

Sam thought of the carved wooden box hidden in her truck. "I wish you could give me some answers."

She scanned the room one last time, then walked down the short hall and took another look into Victor's bedroom. "Where are you, Victor?" she whispered, her voice barely audible. "What mess have you gotten yourself into?"

She turned to leave, a floorboard creaking under her foot, startling her. Her heart thumped as she froze in place, listening for any signs of Rosalita's return. After a moment of tense silence, she exhaled slowly.

"Get it together, Sam," she chided herself. "You're not breaking into houses for a living anymore. This is personal."

At the back door, she hesitated, remembering the recently turned earth in the backyard and the way Rosalita had quickly steered her away from that area. She could call Beau and report it, but he had his hands full right now.

"I'll check it out and call him if there's really anything to report." The doorknob turned smoothly, and she stepped out to the small-screened porch, her eyes searching the yard.

There it was, a spot about ten feet away where the earth was freshly turned. A shovel sat propped against the back of the house, and she carried it with her as she approached. She'd barely scooped out two shovelfuls of dirt when the stench hit her.

Chapter 12

Oh no. Her stomach clenched as she took a few steps back. A flashback—a memory of the first time she'd encountered a buried body behind a house she'd broken into. She shook off the image and turned back to look more closely.

"Okay, Sam, stop and think clearly."

On closer examination, she realized the disturbed patch of ground here was nowhere near large enough for a body. That was something positive. She edged closer and jabbed the shovel into the ground again, holding her breath against the odor. Three more scoops of earth, and she realized what she had here. Garbage.

She pulled away some more dirt and saw that the hole was filled with rotten food—chicken bones, mushy lettuce, tomatoes that were barely recognizable. Rosalita must have cleared out the refrigerator and decided to bury the spoiled food, rather than setting a bag out for the trash collector.

Sam relaxed as she piled the dirt back over the mess, tamping it down and smoothing it. Her Grandma Sweet used to do the same thing with her kitchen scraps. Once, a peach pit had sprouted and grown, to the point where the resulting tree yielded bushels of peaches.

She returned the shovel to the place where she'd found it and rinsed her hands at the garden spigot, brushing them on her jeans to dry them a bit. Retracing her steps into the house, she locked the back door, then the front, as she stepped outside.

"Victor, wherever you are, I hope you're safe. And I hope you've got a damn good explanation for all of this."

It was time to ask more questions. Someone must have seen something. Sam glanced at the surrounding homes as she descended the front steps. She paused on the sidewalk, the mild spring air carrying the scent of blooming forsythia.

Sam scanned the quiet street, her eyes narrowing as she searched for any sign of Rosalita's return. Everything seemed quiet. Satisfied that the coast was clear, she strode purposefully toward her truck.

As she reached for the door handle, a nagging thought stopped her short. "Wait a minute," she muttered.

The memory of a conversation at her bakery floated to the surface. Bertha Gonzales, a regular customer, had offhandedly mentioned to someone in the shop that she was a neighbor of Victor's and had overheard an argument at the Martinez residence. Sam thought fondly of the elderly woman who always seemed to have a bit of gossip to share. Mrs. G seemed like the type who hovered near her windows, proud of the fact that she knew what was going on in her neighborhood.

"I should start there," Sam decided. Pushing off from the truck, she made her way to Bertha's house. Despite being in her late eighties, the old woman kept a meticulously maintained garden, and her spring hyacinths and tulips were a riot of fragrant color surrounding the adobe home.

Squaring her shoulders, Sam knocked, deciding how to broach the subject. After a moment, the door creaked open, revealing Bertha's weathered face and tiny stature.

"Samantha Sweet!" the elderly woman exclaimed, her eyes lighting up. "What a pleasant surprise. Are you making deliveries today?"

Sam smiled warmly, slipping easily into her friendly baker persona. "Not today, Mrs. G. I was actually hoping to chat with you about something I heard. Do you have a moment?"

Bertha nodded, ushering Sam inside. As they settled in the cozy living room, Sam's eyes darted around, taking in the knick-knacks that adorned every surface, the soft throw pillows with homemade covers on them.

"It's about Victor, next door," Sam began carefully, watching the older woman's reaction. "I couldn't help but remember you mentioning some ... disturbance a while back, some kind of a fight? I was wondering if you could tell me more about that?"

Bertha's smile faltered slightly, her gaze dropping to her hands. "Ah, yes. Oh my, it was around Christmas. I remember because my nephews stopped by with a little gift and we were standing out on the porch when they left. It was cold out and I had my blue shawl around me."

"Um, right." Sam kept her voice gentle but probing. "This argument, I think you said it happened next door, at Victor's place?"

"Oh yes." The gray head nodded vigorously.

"Was it between Victor and Rosalita?"

Mrs. G's eyes widened. "Oh, those two—they would go at it sometimes. I wasn't surprised when they divorced, really. But that night last winter…" She pursed her lips, showing a lot of creases. "No … it wasn't them. Rosalita treats me okay, even though she doesn't live there anymore. I have her in, at least once a month, to clean house for me, you know."

"And the argument … at Christmas …"

"Oh yes. No, it wasn't Rosalita, but there was at least one woman, because afterward, when I was back inside, I looked out and saw a woman driving the car."

"Okay … do you remember what the car looked like, the make and model?"

The elderly woman scoffed. "Hah, they all look alike these days. It was white."

"Right. And the woman? Could you describe her?"

"Maybe kind of tall. Of course everyone looks tall to me anymore." She laughed. "She wore a puffy coat and a knitted cap. But it was too dark to see her eyes or her hair. And the same thing with the man."

"Can you describe the man?"

"They were together. His hair was dark. I didn't know either of them."

Sam smiled. That didn't exactly rule out very many people. "And the argument. Could you hear what it was about?"

She shook her head slowly. "Not exact words. The tone seemed threatening, in some way. I don't know. I probably shouldn't have said anything. But I just remember feeling relieved when they left. Victor has always been so quiet …

humble, I guess you would say."

"I know what you mean." Sam stood up and thanked her for the information. "Did you ever bring it up with Victor—the argument?"

"Oh, no. I haven't seen him again since that night. It's when he disappeared."

Further questions didn't bring out anything new. Before she could get roped into staying for coffee, Sam thanked Bertha profusely and left.

She had a sinking feeling in her stomach as she got into her truck and drove away.

Chapter 13

Who could have argued so vehemently with Victor that a neighbor could overhear it? And what was it about that argument that sent him away? Had these visitors actually killed him that night, coming back later to dispose of his body? The questions nagged at her as she drove toward the sheriff's department.

When Sam entered Beau's office, she found him at his desk, tapping a pen against his notebook, his normally calm demeanor replaced by visible frustration. His lean body was taut with tension, and he muttered something under his breath.

"Beau?" Sam called softly.

He looked up, his blue eyes clouded. "Sam, I didn't expect you. I'm just … Never mind."

She could practically feel the waves of impatience

rolling off him. But then he tamped a stack of forms together, pushed his notes aside and stood, stretching. "Sorry I haven't been of more help in locating Victor," he said.

"I might have something," she ventured, knowing how much Beau valued her insights, even if he didn't always understand her methods.

Beau stopped mid-stretch, a glimmer of hope in his eyes. "Sounds good. Want to share?"

"I've been talking to some people, and I think there might be more to Victor's disappearance than we initially thought."

Beau's eyebrows raised, his interest piqued. He gestured toward the chair across from his desk. "Let's hear it."

As they sat down, Sam couldn't help but notice the dark circles under Beau's eyes. "You look exhausted, honey," she said softly.

Beau sighed, running a hand over his face. "We're stretched thin at the moment, and now I have a whole new set of mandates to implement here in my department. I hate to admit it, but I can't give Victor's case full-time attention."

He let out a deep sigh. "I've got a string of burglaries downtown, that drug bust over in El Prado, and now there's talk of some land dispute out by the pueblo. It's like trying to juggle sharp knives while walking a tightrope."

Sam nodded sympathetically, understanding the pressure he was under. "Maybe I shouldn't bother you with this."

A small smile played on Beau's lips. "I respect your insights, darlin'. If you've got something, I'm all ears. Bring me something to act on and I'll do whatever I can to allocate resources to find Victor. He's been a part of this community for too long for me to ignore his disappearance."

Sam's voice became low and intense. "I think someone close to Victor might have betrayed him."

"What makes you think that? In what way?"

"It's … really just a hunch," she said finally, her voice carefully measured. "But my gut tells me that there's more to this than meets the eye."

Beau's eyes locked on hers. "Something to do with that box?"

She tilted her head and gave a little smile. "Maybe a little."

To her surprise, Beau's expression softened. He reached across the desk and took her hand. "Honey, I've seen you solve cases in ways I never could. Whatever methods you're using, I trust you. We're partners in this, remember?"

Sam felt a wave of relief wash over her. "You really mean that?"

Beau nodded, a small smile playing on his lips. "Of course I do. Your intuition has never steered us wrong before. If you think someone close to Victor betrayed him, then that's a lead worth pursuing. Just keep in mind that we need actual evidence before we can make an arrest."

Sam reached into her pocket and pulled out the folded piece of paper. "I've been over to Victor's house, looking for clues, and I found this in his cookbook," she said, smoothing it out on Beau's desk. "It's in Spanish, but I think it might be important. I'd like to get Rico to translate it for me."

Beau rested his forearms on the desk, as he examined the note. "Interesting," he murmured, his eyes scanning the words. "What makes you think this is connected to his disappearance?"

"You should see this cookbook. It's not only recipes. The whole thing is filled with little notations in the margins, a real mix of English and Spanish. A lot of them were unrelated to cooking." Sam was beginning to regret that she hadn't brought the whole book with her.

"And this 'betrayal' … you believe this note might corroborate that?"

Sam nodded. "It's just a hunch, but …"

"Rico!" Beau called out suddenly, his voice carrying through the open office door. The young officer appeared moments later. "Could you take a look at this? We need a translation."

Rico reached for the note as Beau handed it over. "*Ella se lo llevará todo a menos que la detenga.* She will take it all unless you stop her." He handed the note back. "Is this related to one of our cases?"

Sam met his gaze. "I found it at Victor's house. It seems to fit with what I've been thinking about Rosalita, her getting power of attorney and trying to sell his house."

Beau turned back to Sam. "It's circumstantial evidence at best," he said quietly, "but in my experience, seemingly unrelated pieces often form a larger picture in these cases."

Sam felt a surge of affection for her husband. Even when dealing with a dozen different matters at once, he approached everything with the same methodical thoroughness. Rico walked out into the squad room again, taking a phone call at his desk.

Beau was staring at the note again. "This tracks with your theory, Sam," he said, his mind clearly trying to put it together.

"It sure sounds like Victor suspected something wasn't right, but I'm not sure it's the whole story." Sam told him about the neighbor's recollection of a loud argument the night before Victor disappeared. "Beau, we have to find him. He's always been there when anyone needed help, and now he's the one who needs us." Her eyes flashed. "I can't just sit back and do nothing."

Beau nodded, understanding. "I know, honey. And we won't. But we need to tread carefully here. We don't know if we're dealing with kidnapping, foul play, or a man who simply wanted to get out. No matter how it turns out, you don't want to tip your hand too soon."

"I just … I have a strong feeling about this, Beau. Call it women's intuition if you want, but I know something's not right."

Beau reached across the desk, his hand covering hers. "I trust you, Sam. You've got a knack for seeing things others miss. It's one of the reasons I've deputized you before. You keep your ear to the ground in town, and whenever I've got someone available, I'll have my deputies do some quiet digging."

Sam felt a wave of relief wash over her as they stood up. "Thank you," she said softly. "I promise I won't do anything reckless."

Beau gave her a slightly skeptical look, but he pulled her into a hug. "Please don't. You're too important to me."

She stepped back and looked up into his eyes. "Listen, you can't work all night. Let the deputies handle their shifts here, come home for a restful evening, and I'll pick up your favorite chile rellenos for dinner."

"Deal. Home in thirty … make it forty-five minutes."

Samantha set off toward Casa Alvarez, thinking of the conflicting tales she'd heard about Rosalita Suarez. "A dependable house cleaner, sweet as pie, according to some," she mused internally. "A conniving shrew, if you ask others. But which is the truth?"

She parked to the side of the converted hacienda and followed the walkway to the front door, where golden lights illuminated the warm interior. Through the large windows, she saw families seated at the tables in the main dining room. Carlos Alvarez and his wife, Filomena, had purposely kept the restaurant small and the recipes home-cooked. The familiar chatter of locals washed over her when she walked in, a comforting backdrop to her inner turmoil.

She walked up to the counter and placed her order: two chile relleno plates, to go. "They'll be ready in ten minutes," the young clerk assured her. Sam knew the girl was family, probably a granddaughter.

Scanning the room, her eyes landed on a group of regulars clustered around a corner table. At the center sat Filomena Alvarez, her silver hair pulled back in a tight bun, sharp eyes surveying the room over the rim of her coffee cup, as she did most evenings since Carlos had passed.

"Samantha Sweet, it's good to see you again. How is Sheriff Beau?" She gestured toward an empty chair.

"Oh, I don't want to interrupt your group. My order will be ready soon."

"Then sit, take a few minutes to relax. I understand you're working on a new case?"

Nothing gets past anyone in this town, Sam thought. "Yes, it seems like Victor Martinez has just kind of disappeared. I went out to his house and talked to Rosalita a couple of times."

The older woman's expression hardened, her voice dropping to a near-whisper. "That woman? She's as cunning as a fox left to babysit the chickens. Always seems to have an ulterior motive, that one."

"What makes you say that?"

Filomena glanced around, exchanging looks with the others, before continuing, "Mark my words, she's up to something. One day she's crying about her poor, sick husband, the next she's strutting around like she owns the place."

As Filomena spoke, Samantha wished, not for the first time, that her ability to see auras extended to hearing about people secondhand. It would make solving this mystery so much simpler.

"That's … certainly interesting," Samantha mused, keeping her tone neutral. "Have you noticed anything specific that made you suspicious?"

Another woman at the table spoke up. "Let's just say, for someone so 'devoted' to her missing husband, she seems awfully cozy with some man over at the Taoseño in the evenings. And people have seen her coming and going from Victor's house at all hours, always looking over her shoulder like she's got something to hide."

Filomena's gaze drifted to a spot somewhere behind Sam, and another customer walked over, arms open to the owner. The two immediately got into a conversation in rapid Spanish, and Sam excused herself. She stood at the counter for a minute, but the girl who'd taken her order was nowhere to be seen; there was a lot of hustle-bustle going on in the kitchen.

Samantha's eyes drifted across the café, spotting Henry Jenkins, who sat alone at a corner table, his weathered hands wrapped around a steaming mug. The retired schoolteacher's kind eyes crinkled as he nodded a greeting.

Samantha approached, her mind still on Filomena Alvarez's accusations about Rosalita.

"Mind if I join you for a minute, until my order's ready?" she asked, sliding into the chair opposite him.

"Not at all, Samantha. How's the bakery?"

"Busy as ever," she replied with a smile. "How is Mrs. Jenkins these days?"

"Not acting like a retired old lady, that's for sure. She plays canasta once a week with that gang—" he nodded toward Filomena and her cronies. "And she's always off to the grandchildren's ball games or having lunch with one of her former co-workers or something. Tonight, I think it's bowling, but I can't keep track."

Mr. Jenkins took a thoughtful sip of his coffee. "I couldn't help but overhear some of what Filomena was saying just now. You know, I've known Rosalita and Victor for years. Taught his nephew, Marcos, back in the day. Rosalita grew up near Velarde, you know, a little south of here. The Suarez family had nothing, absolutely *nothing*. I always admired Rosalita for her spunk. She worked hard, earned her own way from the time she was about seventeen or so."

"What's your impression of her relationship with Victor? Especially since Victor's disappearance?"

"Well," Mr. Jenkins began, "it's been hard on her, no doubt. I've seen her at the grocery store a few times, looking absolutely distraught. She told me how worried she was about Victor, how she'd been calling doctors in Mexico, trying to get information about his condition."

Samantha's eyebrows rose slightly. This account painted a very different picture from several others. "She seemed genuinely anxious?"

"Oh, absolutely. I could tell she was beside herself. She even mentioned how she was keeping his business going, just in case he came back. Didn't want him to lose everything he'd worked for, you know?"

The disparity between this account and Mrs. Alvarez's was striking. Was Rosalita truly a devoted wife—even as an ex—or a masterful actress? Samantha itched to touch something of Rosalita's and then handle the wooden box, to see if she might gain some insight.

"That's … very different from what I've heard," Samantha admitted, careful not to reveal too much. "Do you think it's possible she might be … putting on an act?"

Mr. Jenkins shook his head firmly. "I've known that woman for decades, Samantha. She's always been devoted to Victor. Sure, they had their squabbles like any couple, but the love was there. I can't imagine her being capable of such lies."

A voice called out.

"Oh—looks like my order is ready." Samantha smiled at him. "Thank you, Mr. Jenkins. You've given me a lot to consider."

Driving north toward home, Sam pondered everything she'd heard and witnessed. She wasn't sure what to believe at this moment. The truth about Rosalita seemed more elusive than ever, a jigsaw puzzle with pieces that refused to fit together. She'd need to dig deeper, she realized, to uncover the real Rosalita Suarez y Martinez.

Chapter 14

Sam woke early the next morning. She and Beau were both exhausted last night and had fallen into bed shortly after dinner. She stretched, feeling amazingly refreshed, then showered and dressed for her day. First on the agenda was to get to the plaza early, to buy a few jars of the local honey that gave the Sweet's Sweets baklava its distinctive flavor. Visiting a popular and crowded venue would also give her a chance to ask whether anyone else had any ideas about where Victor might be.

Leaving her van parked behind Sweet's Sweets, she walked the short distance to the plaza, where a vibrant farmers' market was in full swing. The adobe buildings lining the square seemed to glow in the spring light as Sam weaved through the colorful stalls. The aroma of fresh produce and homemade tortillas mingled with the spicy scent of handcrafted candles.

"Morning, Sam!" called out Hannah de Silva from her tamale stand. "How's business at Sweet's Sweets?"

"Can't complain," Sam replied with a smile, moving closer. "Say, you haven't seen Victor Martinez around lately, have you?"

The negative shake of the head came as no surprise. "Do you know Rosalita Suarez, his ex?"

Hannah's cheerful expression faltered slightly. "Oh, Rosy? Sure, I know her. Why do you ask?"

Sam shrugged casually. "Just curious. There's been some speculation around town, things she has said about Victor and why he's suddenly not around."

"Well," Hannah moved closer, lowering her voice, "between you and me, that woman's got more faces than a deck of cards. Never know which one you're gonna get."

"In what way?"

"Oh, you know. Sometimes I feel like I can trust what she says, and other times … not at all."

Sam nodded, backing away when another customer stepped up and drew Hannah's attention. She continued through the market, her gray hair ruffling in the gentle breeze. She spotted Nick Pearl's vegetable stand and made her way over, her keen eyes noting the tension in his shoulders as she approached.

"Morning, Nick," Sam greeted, picking up a ripe tomato. "How's the harvest this year?"

Nick's weathered face drooped into a frown. "Could be better. That Rosalita's been undercutting my prices again, driving down to Costco in Albuquerque to buy cheap and then reselling the produce to her housekeeping customers. I swear, that woman's out to ruin me."

Sam raised an eyebrow, setting the tomato down. "Oh?

I thought Victor handled the business end of things."

"Ha! That's what she wants everyone to think. And he used to. We got along great because he did his thing and I did mine. We gave each other lots of space. But then Rosalita moves in with her own plans. Mark my words, Sam, that woman's as manipulative as they come. Victor disappears, and suddenly she's running everything? Doesn't add up."

Sam nodded thoughtfully. "You've had run-ins with her before?"

"More times than I can count," Nick growled. "She's always got an angle, always working some scheme, and it's always about making money. I wouldn't trust her as far as I could throw her—and, trust me, that ain't far."

"Thanks for the insight, Nick," she said, selecting a few vegetables to take home and some fruit for the bakery. "I appreciate your honesty."

Sam paid and moved on, wondering if she was missing something crucial. The Rosalita described by Nick seemed worlds apart from the devoted wife Mr. Jenkins had portrayed. Which version was real? Or was the truth, as it so often was, somewhere in the murky middle?

Sam walked through the bustling market, pondering. "Personalities are a tricky thing," she muttered to herself, absently reaching out to touch a display of hand-woven blankets. The smooth texture reminded her of the carved box that had changed her life, awakening abilities she never knew she possessed. Her ability to see fingerprints and auras had been the key to unraveling more than one mystery.

As she strolled up to the stall selling local honey, Maria, the local beekeeper and one of her regular customers at

Sweet's Sweets, approached with a smile. "Hey there, Sam! Taking a break from all that baking?"

Sam smiled, grateful for the distraction. "A very short one. Gotta get back soon. For now, I could use four jars of honey," she replied, keeping her tone light.

Maria pointed out the different varieties, including a spicy one, but Sam decided to go with her usual, not wanting to mess around with a tried-and-true recipe. As she pulled out cash for the purchase, she brought up the subject on her mind. "Say, you've been in Taos a while. What do you know about Rosalita Suarez?"

Maria's expression turned thoughtful. "Rosalita? Well, that's a name that stirs up mixed feelings around here. Why the interest?"

Sam shrugged, aiming for casual. "Oh, mainly I'm just curious. I've been hearing some conflicting stories."

"I bet," Maria chuckled. "That woman's a real enigma. Some swear she's a saint, others say she's the devil incarnate. Me? I think the truth's probably somewhere in between."

Sam nodded, her suspicions confirmed. "Seems to be a pattern. And Victor Martinez, Rosalita's ex—you haven't run into him lately, have you?"

"I wish. He usually comes out to my place and works his magic on the flowering plants. The bees love the result. But no, this year he hasn't come around, and I've been too busy to try and track him down."

Sam nodded. "Thanks, Maria. I should get back to the bakery now, but if you do hear from Victor, please tell him I'm looking for him."

She took the box containing the four jars of honey, looped the bag containing her veggies over her arm, and headed across the middle of the square. As she approached the Plaza gazebo, the sound of youthful laughter drifted toward her. A group of young adults lounged on the grass, their faces animated in conversation. Sam's eyes were drawn to a short, cocky-looking young man at the center of the group. Marcos Sanchez, Victor's nephew who didn't seem to have time to actually get a job.

"Hey guys, how's it going?" She paused and met Marcos's gaze directly. "Oh—Marcos. How are you? Did Rosalita reach out to you about that job?"

The group turned to look at her, curiosity evident in their expressions. Sam introduced herself to the group at large, recognizing a couple of the girls as bakery customers. Marcos put away his sullen expression when a girl nudged him to answer Sam's question.

"Haven't heard from her. I really doubt the bitch wants to be paying me for anything."

"Marcos! That's not really fair," a young woman with kind eyes interjected. "I'm Jasmine," she said to Sam. "And I actually have a story about Rosalita that might surprise you."

Sam turned her attention to Jasmine, noting Marcos's annoyed expression from the corner of her eye. "I'd love to hear it," she encouraged.

Jasmine's voice was soft but earnest. "Last winter, my cousin's family was really struggling. Lost their jobs, couldn't pay rent. Rosalita found out somehow and showed up at their door with groceries and an envelope full of cash. Wouldn't take no for an answer."

Sam's eyebrows rose. This certainly didn't fit with the manipulative image others had painted of Rosalita. "That's incredibly generous," she said, working to reconcile this new information.

Marcos sneered. "Yeah, well, one good deed doesn't make her a saint. Rosalita isn't always what she seems. She's got her own agenda, trust me."

The atmosphere was becoming a little prickly, so Sam edged her way out of the group. She couldn't help but wonder about the history between Marcos and his uncle Victor. The pieces of the puzzle were starting to form a more complex picture, but the edges were still blurry.

As she walked away from the gazebo, the comments swirled through her head. Rosalita's character seemed more nuanced than ever. Was she a manipulative schemer or a secret philanthropist? She wished she'd handled the carved box ahead of time as she'd spoken to all these various people, to glimpse the truth behind their stories. But for now, she'd have to rely on good old-fashioned detective work—and maybe a batch of her famous lemon bars to loosen a few more tongues around town.

Sam's footsteps echoed on the sidewalk as she made her way back to Sweet's Sweets, the adobe buildings surrounding the plaza casting long shadows in the early morning sun. Like Rosalita, Taos had many faces—traditional and modern, spiritual and practical.

"Truth is never simple," she muttered to herself. "Especially when someone's working hard to hide it." Her mind refused to slow down, and the variety of conversations she'd had in the past few days echoed through her brain like a movie on an endless loop.

A warm breeze carried the scent of sage, reminding Sam of the complexity of her adopted hometown. As she approached her bakery, Sam paused to enjoy her window display. The familiar sight of Sweet's Sweets always brought comfort.

Sam pushed open the door, the cheerful bell tinkling overhead. The comforting aroma of the cheeses in Julio's special quiche enveloped Sam as she stepped inside.

"Hey, Sam!" Jen's cheerful voice cut through her musings. "How was your walk?"

Sam blinked, refocusing on her surroundings. Jen stood behind the counter, her dark hair neatly tucked into its usual bun, a warm smile on her face.

"I got several jars of our favorite honey, plus some beautiful fruit," Sam replied, her tone distracted. She glanced around the bakery, noting a couple of regulars enjoying coffee and pastries. "The walk itself was … interesting. How's it been here?"

As Jen showed her the receipts from the morning sales so far, Sam found her attention drifting. She nodded absently, replaying snippets of conversations in her head, both from the café last night and the farmers' market this morning.

Mrs. Alvarez thinks she's cunning … Mr. Jenkins says she's devoted … Nick Pearl doesn't trust her at all, Sam mused internally. *And then there's Jasmine's story of generosity. Who is the real Rosalita?*

"Sam? Did you hear me?" Jen's voice broke through her reverie.

"I'm sorry, Jen. What was that?" Sam shook her head, trying to clear it.

"I said we're running low on those new raspberry tarts. They've been really popular."

"Right, of course," Sam nodded, moving toward the kitchen. "I bought raspberries, and I'll get started on them right away."

"One step at a time," she reminded herself a few

minutes later as she measured butter and sugar, blending in the flour for the crusts. "There's a truth hidden in this mystery, and I'm going to find it."

Chapter 15

The bell above the door of Sweet's Sweets jingled, and Samantha looked up from the finished raspberry tarts she was arranging in the display case to see Rosalita striding in, a crumpled letter clutched in her hand. The older woman's black hair gleamed dully under the soft bakery lights, and her presence seemed to fill the entire entryway.

"Samantha Sweet," Rosalita called out, her voice carrying a sharp edge. "We need to talk."

Sam's eyebrows shot up, and she quickly scanned the sales area. Empty, save for Jen behind the register. Thank goodness, she thought, though her heart thumped at the unexpected confrontation.

"Of course, Rosalita," Sam replied, keeping her voice steady. "Why don't we sit down?" She gestured to one of the bistro tables near the window, where the warm sun streamed in, casting long shadows across the hardwood floorboards.

As they moved to the table, Sam caught Jen's eye and gave a subtle nod toward the kitchen. The young woman understood immediately, disappearing through the curtain with a soft whoosh.

Once seated, Rosalita didn't waste any time. "I received a threatening letter. I think it's because of you asking questions, spreading rumors about me."

Sam held out a hand. "May I see it?"

Rosalita handed over the letter, watching carefully as Sam's eyes scanned the page. It was a simple message, written in an immature scrawl: *You have no right to Victor's money or his things. Back off. Let him come home.*

"Who sent this, Rosalita?"

"*You* didn't?" The older woman's expression cycled through anger and indignation, and finally settled on a mask of innocence that didn't quite work.

Sam sat up straighter and passed the letter back across the table. "I did not. Surely you know that. So, who else would think you are possibly helping yourself to Victor's belongings?"

"I have no idea who would accuse me of dishonesty," Rosalita said, her voice dripping with insincerity. "You know me, Samantha. I'm an open book."

Sam fought the urge to roll her eyes. An open book with half the pages torn out and the rest written in invisible ink, maybe, she thought. Aloud, she said, "So you have no idea who might have sent this?"

As Rosalita launched into a long-winded explanation about her innocence and how shocked she was by such accusations, Sam recalled the conflicting stories she'd heard from this woman—sometimes Victor was ill in Mexico, sometimes just away on business. The ever-changing narrative about power of attorney and the landscape business. Each tale more improbable than the last, and several of them directly contradicted by others.

Sam took a deep breath; this would be a frustrating conversation. She had a feeling that getting to the truth with Rosalita would be like trying to nail Jello to the wall, but she had to try.

"Rosalita," Sam interrupted gently, "I understand this must be upsetting. But, considering that no one knows what has happened with Victor, surely you can see why people might be getting alarmed?"

Rosalita's pseudo-smile slipped for just a moment, revealing a flash of something harder underneath. "What exactly are you implying, Samantha?" she asked, her tone once again frosty.

Sam chose her next words carefully, all too aware of the delicate balance she was trying to maintain. "I'm not implying anything. I'm just trying to understand the situation. There have been a lot of different stories going around about when and where Victor went and whether his business affairs are being handled. I hope you might be able to clear things up."

Rosalita's eyes narrowed, and Sam could almost see the gears turning behind them, calculating her next move in this verbal chess match.

Samantha rested her elbows on the polished surface of the bistro table. "Rosalita," Sam said, her voice gentle but firm, "where *exactly* is Victor now? And how is he doing?"

Rosalita's expression hardened, her lips pressed into a thin line. "As I've told everyone who's asked, Victor is in Mexico," she snapped, her attitude becoming defensive.

"He's recovering from a very serious illness. It's been … difficult."

"So you've said. When was the last time you heard from him?"

Rosalita's eyes darted away for a split second. "It's been … well, we communicate regularly."

Sam saw an opening and decided to press further. "That's good to hear. Are there some messages or emails you could show me? It might help put people's minds at ease."

Rosalita hesitated, her stubby fingers drumming nervously on the table. Sam could almost see the internal struggle playing out behind those dark eyes. Finally, Rosalita let out a resigned sigh.

"Fine," she said, reaching for her purse. "I suppose I can show you some of our text messages. But I'm telling you, there's nothing suspicious going on here."

As Rosalita fumbled with her phone, Sam wondered— would they bring her any closer to uncovering the full truth?

Rosalita finally found the right screen and handed the phone over to Sam, who gripped the gaudy rhinestone case.

Sam's eyes narrowed as she scrolled through the message thread, conversation bubbles of Spanish text filling the screen. Her limited grasp of the language left her feeling frustrated and out of her depth. She recognized a few words here and there—"amor," "familia," "Mexico"— but the context eluded her.

She glanced up at Rosalita, whose face had settled into an impassive mask. "Could you translate some of these for me?"

Rosalita's long hair fell across her shoulder. "Of course," she said, her voice dripping with artificial sweetness. "This one here, Victor says he's feeling much better. The Mexican air is doing wonders for his health."

As Rosalita continued to narrate, Sam watched her body language. Something about the way Rosalita tapped nervously on the phone screen didn't sit right with her.

"And here," Rosalita pointed to another message, "Victor talks about how much he misses me, how he wants us to get back together. He says he's thinking of the good times we had."

Sam nodded. It almost seemed like the woman was making up the narrative as she went, a story that seemed plausible on the surface, but as she asked a question now and then, there were inconsistencies that nagged at her. Dates that didn't quite line up, references to events that seemed out of place for a man supposedly recovering from a serious illness.

"That's ... interesting," Sam said carefully, tilting her head. "It's good to hear he's doing better. Has he mentioned when he might return to Taos?"

Rosalita stammered a little, and Sam pressed harder.

"Rosalita," Sam began, her voice steady despite the tension coiling in her stomach, "these messages ... are you certain they're from Victor?"

Rosalita's eyes flashed. "What are you saying?" she snapped. "Of course they're from Victor! You think I would lie about my husband's condition?"

Sam held up a placating hand. "I'm not accusing you of anything. It's just that in my experience, sometimes people can impersonate others in text messages. I want to make sure Victor is really okay, that these messages are truly coming from him."

Rosalita's nostrils flared, her round face indignant. "Victor is fine! He's in Mexico, recovering, just like I said. How dare you suggest otherwise!"

Sam held up a hand. "Hold on. I understand you're upset, but please, help me understand. You mentioned earlier that you're managing Victor's affairs. Does that include selling his home? If he's coming back, he would not want the house sold."

Rosalita's eyes darted away for a moment, and Sam felt a flicker of triumph. She was onto something.

"What does that matter?" Rosalita huffed, crossing her arms over her chest.

Sam's voice dropped to a conspiratorial whisper. "I'm just trying to piece everything together. You mentioned that you are handling his business, hiring some young people to do the work. But I ran into Marcos this morning and he denies working for you."

"Well, it's not Marcos working for me, after all. Lazy kid. I've found others." Rosalita launched into a convoluted explanation about subcontractors and temporary arrangements. Sam listened intently, noting every contradiction and evasion. The more Rosalita talked, the more Sam became convinced that the truth about Victor's disappearance was far more complex than a simple trip to Mexico.

Rosalita's face contorted, her friendly expression vanishing as she slammed her palm on the table. "Enough! This is none of your business, Samantha Sweet. You're just a nosy baker who should stick to her pastries!"

Sam remained outwardly calm. She'd struck a nerve. "Rosalita, I'm only trying to help. If Victor's really okay—"

"I don't need your help!" Rosalita snarled. "You think you're so clever with your little questions, but you're meddling in things you don't understand."

"I understand that a man is missing, and his ex-wife's story doesn't add up."

Rosalita's eyes narrowed dangerously. "Are you calling me a liar?"

"I'm saying there are inconsistencies," Sam replied evenly. "We could clear it up right now. Call Victor and let me talk to him."

"Fine." Rosalita jerked the phone back and tapped some numbers.

Sam waited patiently, watching the other woman's nervous expression.

"There's no answer. He is probably resting."

"Give me his number."

"It's a Mexican cell phone. The cost of a call will be quite expensive for you."

"I don't mind. I just want to hear his voice and know that he's safe."

Rosalita's expression fumbled. She pretended to scroll through her contacts. "*Mierda*—I've lost it. Erased."

Right. The two women stared at each other, the tension sparking like lightning in the sunlit bakery. Sam knew she wouldn't get anything more from Rosalita today. With a sigh, she stood up, smoothing her baker's jacket.

"I think we're done here," Sam said, gesturing toward the door. "Thank you for your time, Rosalita, and I'm sorry I couldn't answer your question about who sent that letter to you."

Rosalita stomped toward the door, muttering in rapid-fire Spanish. As Sam watched the door close, she was already thinking ahead. She needed to talk to Beau. If they could get warrants for those text messages, maybe they could finally unravel this situation. But she wasn't certain she had adequate grounds.

Sam watched through the bakery's large front window as Rosalita stomped out to her little white car and got in.

"Good riddance," Sam muttered under her breath. As Rosalita started her car and backed out of the lot, Sam watched her drive away. There was more to this story than she'd managed to dig out yet.

Jen poked her head out from the kitchen. "Everything okay, boss?"

Sam nodded, her eyes still fixed on Rosalita's departing vehicle. "Yeah, just … ugh, that woman. Hey, can you hold down the fort for a bit? I need to make a call."

"Sure thing," Jen replied, putting on her smile when a customer walked in.

Sam retreated to the alley behind the bakery, grabbing deep breaths of fresh air. Pulling out her cell phone, she dialed a familiar number.

"Beau? It's me," she said when her husband answered.

She recounted her conversation with Rosalita, including her impression that Rosalita was making up the content of the text messages and outright lying when she said she'd just lost Victor's number from her contact list. "I know we can't just accuse her without proof. But there's got to be a way to verify those messages, right? Maybe a warrant?"

He seemed to be considering the idea, but Sam realized he'd been interrupted by one of his deputies. She listened intently but couldn't pick up much of their conversation.

"Okay, Walters, I'll be right there," he said. "Sorry, darlin' I gotta go. Someone reported a body in the Cooper

Ravine, off the ski valley road."

"Beau …?"

"I don't know what to think yet," he muttered, almost to himself. "Lord, don't let it be Victor."

Chapter 16

Sam knew where the Cooper Ravine was. She'd been involved in a case with some kids who got horribly lost on their ski trip and nearly went off the road there. She pictured the curve in the road, the steep drop-off, and remembered that one of her recent witnesses had said he saw Victor on the ski valley road last December.

What if …?

The thought of their friend lying in a ravine all this time made her feel physically ill.

She dashed into the kitchen, pulling her baker's jacket off as she went. "Becky, Beau just got a call—I need to be with him right now."

"Oh, God, Sam. Is he okay?"

"Yeah, sorry to scare you. It's department business." She grabbed her bag from the wall hook and left the baker's jacket behind.

Pulling out of the alley and heading north on Camino de la Placita, she saw flashing lights ahead. Beau's cruiser and another—probably Rico—had just left the sheriff's department and were only a couple blocks ahead of her.

She kept a steady speed as they passed the turnoff to the pueblo and drove through El Prado. By the time Beau's department vehicles made the turn east toward the mountain, she was right behind them.

She found herself imagining her husband's viewpoint on all this. Beau had known Victor for years, had shared beers with him at the local cantina, had even hired him to fix up the casita on their property two summers ago.

"Keep it together, Sam," she muttered to herself. "You know Beau is the sheriff first, friend second."

But she knew it wasn't that simple. In a town like Taos, where everyone knew everyone, the lines between duty and personal relationships often blurred.

The flashing lights ahead of her traveled in a slow, orderly fashion, and she realized there was no rush if the person who'd been found was already dead. Her throat tightened at the thought.

"If it is Victor," she mused aloud, her voice barely audible over the wail of the sirens, "what the hell happened to him? And why is Rosalita going through the elaborate pretense that he's alive and well in Mexico?" It could only mean one thing. Rosalita was, indeed, planning to cash in on Victor's life achievements.

As Beau pulled up to the scene, his official mask slipped firmly into place. He stepped out of his vehicle and settled his hat in place, the crunch of gravel under his boots punctuating the tense atmosphere. His practiced eye scanned the scene, taking in the positions of his deputies as they secured the perimeter with yellow crime scene tape. Sam felt a surge of pride, watching him at work.

A small cluster of onlookers had already gathered at the edge of the restricted area, their hushed whispers carrying on the mild spring breeze. Sam recognized a few faces—Betty Hansen, a customer from the bakery, old Mr. Ramirez leaning on his cane. Their presence was a stark reminder of how quickly news traveled around here.

Sam got out of her van and walked toward Beau. He'd already spotted her, and his expression was somewhere between frustration and relief. "Sam … you really needed to be here?"

"I couldn't stay back. Sorry. Assign me something to do."

"At this moment, just don't head down there. Stick with me and I'll see if—"

"Sheriff!" Deputy Harris called out, striding toward Beau with a grim expression. "We've got the area locked down."

Beau nodded, going into full official mode. "What have we got, Harris?"

As they walked toward the edge of the arroyo, Harris briefed him. "Male victim, discovered by a couple of hikers about an hour ago. No ID on the body yet."

"Any signs of foul play?" Beau asked, his voice low and measured.

Harris hesitated. "Hard to say, sir. The body's in pretty rough shape. Looks like it's been out here for a while."

Beau's jaw tightened imperceptibly. "What steps have you taken so far?"

"We've photographed the scene, sir," Harris replied.

"Forensics is on their way. We're waiting on the medical investigator before moving the body."

"Good work," Beau nodded, his tone conveying approval despite the gravity of the situation. He glanced back at the growing crowd of onlookers. "Make sure we keep those folks at a distance. Last thing we need is contamination of the scene or wild rumors spreading through town."

As Harris moved to reinforce the perimeter, Beau and Sam stood at the edge of the arroyo. She looked up at his face, set in firm lines now. "Beau, are you thinking about Vic—"

"We all are, Sam. But we can't afford to let personal feelings cloud our judgment. Focus on the facts," he reminded her. "One step at a time."

He turned to face her squarely. "You wait here."

"Beau, I can handle—"

"You don't have adequate footwear for the terrain, and I can't afford to have anyone hurt while we do this."

The words stung, but he was right. She bit her lip and stayed back, watching as Beau carefully made his way down the slope of the arroyo, his boots sounding against the rocky slope. As he approached the body, he pulled a kerchief from his pocket and held it to his nose. Then he paused, taking in the scene.

Sam became aware of Rico, standing beside her. "Can I borrow your binoculars?"

He gave a little sigh and handed over the small pair he carried. Sam held them to her eyes and adjusted the focus.

The victim lay face down, partially obscured by scrub brush. She could see a faded denim jacket, worn work boots, and dark hair peppered with gray. Her heart fluttered in her chest.

"Damn," she muttered, watching as Beau crouched beside the body. "Sure looks like it could be Victor."

She thought of Victor's ready smile, his accented English, the mix of words they jokingly called Spanglish. Tears pricked at her eyes as she pushed the image away, forcing herself to hand the binoculars back to Rico. The young deputy side-stepped his way down the slope.

Within a minute Deputy Harris walked over to stand beside Sam, his eyes scanning the growing crowd and the vehicles behind them.

"I walked down there when I first arrived," he said. "The victim had no wallet, and it looks like he's been out here a while."

"Could you tell—?"

He shook his head. "No way to say for sure who it is. The head injuries from the fall, and the elements … He's not identifiable." He straightened, noting the arrival of another vehicle. "Wait here, Sam."

She recognized the familiar van from the county's only forensic examiner.

"Sheriff?" Deputy Harris called down the slope. "Lisa's here."

Beau stood, brushing dirt from his knees. "Send her down," he replied, his voice remarkably steady.

Please, Sam thought, don't let it be him.

Beau stepped away from the body as the forensic examiner arrived at the bottom of the ravine, and a murmur of voices from the growing crowd grew louder. Sam knew Beau must have heard them; he glanced up. Part of Sam wanted to visit among them, but she knew they would have questions that she really shouldn't answer. She forced herself to merely eavesdrop.

"I heard it's Victor Martinez," a woman's voice carried on the breeze. "Poor Rosalita must be beside herself."

"Nah, can't be," another voice chimed in.

"How do you know?"

But the answer was lost on the breeze. Sam frowned, recognizing the rapid spread of speculation. Beau would need to address the crowd soon. She watched him make his way up the slope, as the crime scene tech began her work. When he reached the top, he walked over to Sam.

"Is it him?"

Beau sighed. "We don't know yet. Have to let the forensic evidence get collected, and there'll be an autopsy."

"Oh, Beau," Sam's voice softened. "How are you holding up?"

"I'm all right," he assured her, his tone gentler than any of his deputies would recognize. "Just trying to keep it together for everyone else."

"You always do," Samantha replied, a hint of pride in her voice, despite the fact that her own insides were churning.

He straightened his shoulders, slipping back into his role as sheriff. It was time to face the crowd and the long day ahead.

Beau had just finished announcing to the crowd that he could not yet speak as to the identity of the person below or what had caused the death—people just needed to go home and wait to hear news after the formal investigation was concluded—when a sleek black SUV pulled up to the scene, its tires crunching on the dirt berm where the other vehicles waited. Doctor Sylvia Lopez, the medical investigator from the county office, stepped out, her dark hair pulled back in a tight bun. Beau strode over to meet her, his boots kicking up small clouds of dust.

"Morning, Doc," Beau greeted, his voice steady despite the tension in his jaw. "Appreciate you coming out so quickly. You remember my wife and sometimes-deputy, Samantha?"

"Hi, Sam. Good to see you again. Or … sorry, not that this is anything good."

As Doctor Lopez stared down toward the body, Beau filled her in on the details. "And we've got a missing person case that might be related."

"Victor Martinez?" Sylvia asked, her eyebrow raised.

Beau nodded, a flicker of surprise crossing his face. "Word travels fast in Taos County."

"Small towns," Doctor Lopez replied with a wry smile. She headed down the hillside. "Let's see what we can learn."

Sam touched Beau's arm. "Shall I …?"

"You don't have to hang around," he said. "It's gonna be a long day, I'm afraid. The body will have to be transported to the OMI in Albuquerque for a full report, and we may not learn anything definite for a day or two. I can fill you in when I get home."

She didn't want to leave, not having answers. But she also knew how these things went, investigations that moved at a snail's pace.

Reluctantly, she trudged back to her van and drove to Sweet's Sweets. She busied herself with mundane tasks that didn't require a lot of concentration or creativity— spreading chocolate icing on a large panful of brownies, dusting the lemon bars with powdered sugar, carrying completed trays of cookies to the display cases out front. Her crew could tell Sam was preoccupied, and they guessed the reason, so they left her alone.

A very long three hours later, her phone pinged with a text message: Holding a briefing in my office. If you want you can attend.

Sam wondered if the news would be good or bad. Stop it, she chided. A body was found. There was no way it was good news. But attending the briefing would give her more of an inside picture of what was going on, plus it would save Beau from having to repeat everything later in the evening.

When she arrived at the sheriff's department, the employee lot was full. He'd scheduled the briefing to coincide with the shift change, another way to avoid having to repeat himself. Sam parked on the street nearby and walked up, using the back door where the deputies came and went. The squad room was full, with every desk and extra chair occupied. She tucked herself into a corner and gave Beau a small wave through the window to his private office.

He emerged a minute later, holding a sheaf of papers. When he cleared his throat, all chatter in the room stopped. He made eye contact with Rico, with Harris, and finally with Sam.

"By now, everyone knows that the body of a deceased individual was discovered this morning by some hikers in Cooper Ravine." He went through the details Sam already knew. "Based on evidence and conditions, it is estimated the victim had been in the location through the winter months, probably at least from last December. Because of cold weather and freezing conditions until more recently, decomposition was not as advanced as it might have been during warmer weather."

Several deputies were taking notes. Some wore pained expressions.

"Doctor Lopez found evidence of maltreatment, possibly foul play, in the form of bruising around the neck and wrists. Understand, because of the slowed decomposition, we do not know with any certainty, how long ago these injuries happened, or if they happened a long time or short time before the death."

He looked up and surveyed the room. "The existence of the injuries is one of those facts we want kept away from the media and the public. Also, a small pocketknife was found nearby. It's not a murder weapon, but could have been a personal possession of either the victim or the killer." He held up a little evidence bag. "You know the drill—do not discuss or reveal those facts to anyone you interview in conjunction with this case."

"As far as the subject's identity … we do not know it at this time."

Sam heard a dozen people exhale at once.

"There was no identification on the body, and it will take some time for the forensic team and medical investigator to learn who our victim was, if they can. Doctor Lopez did point out a small tattoo near the collarbone, something that appears to perhaps be a religious icon—something like a cross, but not exactly that either. There's a photograph and a sketch, which will be handed out, along with the other data points, for you to study."

Sam's mind skimmed over this last bit. Did Victor have any tattoos? She didn't recall ever seeing one, but he'd been a modest man who didn't remove his shirt when he worked, even on the hottest days. She supposed there might be one on his collarbone area.

"At this point, we're considering this to be a John Doe and the cause of death to be homicide. That is, unless we learn differently from the medical investigator's autopsy results in Albuquerque."

He paused a moment and looked at his paperwork again. "Meanwhile, Rico and Walters, I'd like for you to review every missing person case we currently have on the books. I've recently looked at them—yes, Sam, I'll get to that one in a minute—and I don't think we have a match, but I could have missed something. Things were a little disorganized this last fall."

He was referring to the fact that he'd only recently come back onto the job after being 'retired' for a couple of years. Evan Richards might have taken reports that Beau wasn't aware of.

"Sam, I know you and half the people in this room are thinking of Victor Martinez. Do we have any way to get something with his DNA? It would need to come from a confirmed source."

Sam felt all eyes land on her. She shook her head. "I was at Victor's home recently and discovered that his personal belongings are gone. So, no hairbrush, toothbrush, that kind of thing. We might be able to get fingerprints …"

Beau was shaking his head. "Sad to say, the body isn't in good enough condition to yield good enough ones for comparison." He paused to let that sink in. "And there were too many injuries to the face—he's not recognizable. Getting next of kin to identify him won't be possible."

Sam felt deflated. What could they do?

"Meanwhile, the clothing will be scrutinized for clues. Please, give it some thought, everyone, as to what other means we might use for identity purposes." He looked around the room. "Meanwhile, take one of the fact sheets I've got here. Memorize details and be alert for anything pertinent."

As the sheets were passed around the room, someone piped up, a female deputy who recently started on the job. "I recognize the tattoo," she said.

"Oh? You know who had it?"

"No, I just recognize the design. My brother has one like it, the mark of Los Hermanos de Velarde. It's a little symbol of their unity, somewhat religious but not in the traditional sense. It isn't commonly known, so if our victim has this tattoo, he's a member."

"That's good to know. Thank you, Delila. All right, everyone, back to work."

Sam thought back over the years she'd known Victor Martinez. Had he ever talked about being a member of Los Hermanos? She couldn't recall. But she did know who to ask.

Unfortunately, the last time she'd seen the woman things had gotten a little confrontational.

Chapter 17

The department meeting broke up, and Sam followed Beau into his office. "Do you plan to bring Rosalita in, ask her to identify the body?"

He shook his head. "As we discovered, it's not in good enough condition. I was thinking, since you know her, maybe you could go by and ask her about the tattoo—if you can spare the time?"

His thinking tracked so closely with hers, it was almost scary. She reached out and took his hand, giving a squeeze. "Sure. I can do that."

He reached into his desk drawer and pulled out a badge. "Raise your right hand." He quickly ran through the brief swearing-in, and Sam was once again a temporary deputy. "Maybe this will help open some doors."

She stuffed the badge wallet into her bag, gave him

a quick kiss, and was out the door. Fifteen minutes later, she was pulling up at the address he'd given her, a modest adobe house on the southwest end of town. Unlike Victor's place, the yard and flower beds were in good repair here. Maybe Rosalita actually had hired some workers and had them start with her own place.

Sam walked up to the bright blue front door, slipping her hand into the side pocket of her bag and touching the badge. Just in case.

Rosalita answered almost immediately after Sam's knock, her ready smile turning into a firm, straight line when she realized who it was.

"I've told you what I know, Señora Samantha, and this is getting old, having you interrupting my day."

Sam pulled out the wallet and flipped it open to show the badge. "This time it's official, and I just have a couple questions that should be easy enough. May I come in?"

Clearly, Rosalita thought about refusing but the sight of a neighbor, walking to the road with a trash bag in hand, quickly changed her mind. "Put the badge away and come inside," she hissed.

Sam stepped into a small living room, presently cluttered with several familiar-looking boxes. An open archway on her right revealed the kitchen, where a stack of papers sat on the worn wooden table. Her eyes darted across the documents. Some looked like bank statements, others looked like legal papers, but she was too far away to see details.

Rosalita quickly steered her toward the sofa in the living room, her gaze drifting to a framed photo of herself and Victor, smiling in a restaurant somewhere. Sam had to admit they seemed like a happy couple in that time and place. It made her questions all the more difficult.

"Can we sit down a minute?" Sam asked. She took a spot at one end of the worn leather couch. Rosalita opted for a stiff chair beside the kiva fireplace.

"Sheriff Cardwell sent me. There was, um, a body discovered this morning. It's a man about Victor's size and build."

"I heard." She remained remarkably composed.

This town. It seemed there was little use for a newspaper or radio station.

"Right. So, you may have also heard that we haven't been able to identify him yet, and the, uh, elements have not been kind." Sam pulled out the sheet Beau had handed out, the one with the picture of the tattoo. "Do you recognize this?"

"Si. It is the symbol of Los Hermanos de Velarde."

"So, Victor had one like this?"

Rosalita tsked. "No, silly. I come from Velarde, so I have seen this mark, but Victor did not. My husband has no tattoos."

Sam released a pent-up breath. "Oh, thank goodness. It's not him."

"How often must I repeat that Victor is alive and well?"

As often as it takes, until you let me speak with him. She was about to pose the question again, about calling Victor, but Rosalita had risen from her seat, clearly ready to show Sam the door.

"One more thing before I go," Sam said. "I see that you have the boxes of paperwork from Victor's house. His business files, I'm guessing?"

A curt nod.

"We need to look over Victor's appointment calendar for the past year. Someone among his customers—" She halted. Why was she explaining all this to the woman who was only going to stonewall her with the same worn-out story? "You know what—I'll just go. I can have Beau get a warrant for everything we need, and then some."

Rosalita's eyes turned hard as flint. "Fine."

She left the door standing open and marched over to one of the boxes in a stack near the front window. Reaching inside and shuffling through the papers, she pulled out a spiral-bound datebook. "I will get copies of the pages you want and drop them by at the bakery."

Sam opened her mouth to suggest she take the whole book and copy the pages herself, but Rosalita held the book tightly to her chest. "Okay. Can you get them to me before the end of the business day?"

The woman didn't look happy about the whole thing, but she was interrupted by the ringing of her phone. She turned her back on Sam, to take the call.

"*Buenas tardes*, Mr. Thompson," she answered, her voice dripping with honey. "What a pleasure to hear from you again."

Sam caught her attention, pointed at her wrist, and raised a hand with five fingers spread, a reminder about making the copies before the end of the day. Rosalita gave an eye-roll and headed for the kitchen table, settling into a chair and flipping through some papers as she continued her conversation. Sam turned toward the open front door but halted in her tracks at Rosalita's next words.

"Oh, *sí*, the property is still available," she purred. "Victor would be so pleased to know it's going to someone who appreciates its potential."

Sam ducked out of sight behind the dividing wall and froze in place.

The caller's voice came over the speaker. "And Mr. Martinez is okay with the sale? I'd hate to proceed if he's not fully on board."

"*Por supuesto*, of course he is. My poor Victor, he's been so ill lately. That's why I'm handling everything, you see. He trusts me completely with these affairs."

She paused, allowing a hint of consideration to creep into her tone. "In fact, he's staying with family in Mexico right now, getting the best care possible. It's been so difficult, but we must move on, no?"

As Mr. Thompson expressed his sympathy, Sam heard Rosalita riffling through pages, tamping them into place.

"Now, about the offer," Rosalita interjected, a note of steel entering her voice. "I'm sure we can come to an agreement that benefits everyone. Victor's medical bills are adding up."

"I'll have a purchase agreement drafted and sent over to you by tomorrow," the man assured her.

Rosalita ended the call with a saccharine "*Gracias*, Mr. Thompson. We will be in touch."

Sam slid out the open front door and hurried to her van.

Chapter 18

It was mid-afternoon when Sam sensed movement outside the bakery's front window and looked up from the display case she was arranging to see Beau step inside. His khaki sheriff's uniform was wrinkled, and his expression seemed serious. Sam's heart quickened at the sight of her husband, but his serious demeanor sent a flutter of apprehension through her chest.

Sam tried to keep her tone light. "Long day, huh?"

Beau's lips quirked in a small smile, but it didn't reach his eyes as he took in the crowded bakery. "You could say that. Got a minute to talk?"

Sam nodded, wiping her hands on her apron. "Of course. Let me just finish up here."

She carefully placed the last few éclairs in the case. As she closed the glass door, she caught sight of her reflection—her ruffled gray hair, the fine lines around her eyes. For a moment, she wished she could see beyond her own image, to glimpse whatever was weighing on Beau's mind.

"All set," she said, turning to face him.

Beau gently took her elbow, guiding her toward the door. "Let's take a walk."

As they stepped out into the warm afternoon sun, Sam could feel tension radiating from her husband. They crossed the parking lot and headed toward the crosswalk that led to the plaza.

"You got my text, right?"

"I did. About Victor having no tattoos. Sorry I didn't even find a moment to respond."

"I know. Now that we're certain it isn't Victor, it means you have a John Doe murder to solve." It meant she would largely be looking into Victor's disappearance on her own. But that was fine. She could do it, even if the Easter holiday rush delayed her efforts.

They crossed the street and walked along the sidewalk that led into the plaza itself.

"While I was talking to Rosalita, after the briefing, I requested Victor's client list and his schedule for last fall and winter. Figured I might find some other people to interview. Surely, he said something to someone about not feeling well—if that's true—or about planning a trip away. I'm hoping someone knows where he went and has his contact information."

The shops circling the plaza were busy, the sidewalks crowded, so Beau steered their path toward the grassy center of the square. When they came to an unoccupied wrought iron bench, he pulled her down to sit beside him and turned toward her.

"Sam," Beau began, his voice low and measured, "I've got something you need to hear. Rosalita's lawyer sent over a legal warning today. They're demanding you stop your investigation into Victor's disappearance. Technically, I'm here to serve you."

Sam's breath caught in her throat as she took the folded paper he held out to her.

"A legal warning?" Sam whispered. "On what grounds?"

She glanced around the plaza, suddenly hyper-aware of the meandering crowds, recalling her recent conversations with various suspects, including the ever-changing attitude from Rosalita herself.

Beau shook his head slightly. "They're claiming harassment. It's mostly posturing, a basic 'cease and desist' warning, but it's clear Rosalita's getting nervous about something."

"I think I know what it is. I overheard part of a phone call when I was at her house earlier, a Mr. Thompson who sounds serious about buying Victor's house. Rosalita said something about looking forward to receiving his written offer."

"Hm. To proceed with that, she would need Victor's power of attorney. I'm guessing she actually did get that."

"What do you think, Beau?" she asked, searching his face. "As my husband, not as the sheriff."

Beau's eyes softened, and he took her hand in his. "As your husband, I'm asking you to be careful. Rosalita's probably not doing this on her own. If she's working in tandem with someone with lots of money, then she's not one to be trifled with, and this feels like more than just a scare tactic. But I also know how important this is to you, and to Victor's many friends."

Sam nodded, feeling the warmth of Beau's hand.

Beau sighed, his sheriff's uniform crinkling with the movement. "Sam, Rosalita's lawyer isn't messing around. They're threatening a lawsuit if you don't back off."

"So, I'd need a lawyer. Both to defend anything she wants to say about me, but to stop her from selling Victor's house until we can find out if that's truly his wish?"

"Honey," Beau said, his voice low and laced with protectiveness, "I think it's time you consider stepping back from this investigation. For your own safety." His earnest blue eyes met hers. "We don't know what kind of trouble you might be stirring up here. She may have resources we can't even imagine, depending on who else is possibly behind this. They could try to sue you for everything you've got."

Sam's mind whirled, torn between her innate desire to uncover the truth and the very real threat now looming over her. She thought of Sweet's Sweets, of the life she and Beau had built together.

"But Victor," she began, her voice catching. "We can't just let this go, can we? After everything ..."

Beau's expression softened, but his grip tightened. "I know how much this means to you, Sam. But we're talking about your livelihood here, maybe even more. These aren't the kind of people you want to tangle with."

Sam's gaze drifted across the surrounding shops, taking in the familiar adobe buildings—the hotel, the mercantile, and the many galleries—bathed in the warm afternoon light. She had a whirlwind of questions and doubts. Why was Rosalita trying to shut down her investigation? What was the cunning woman hiding, besides wanting to make a ton of money by selling the house?

The consequences of pushing forward loomed large in Sam's mind. Her bakery, the dream she'd worked so hard to achieve, could be at risk. And yet, the image of Victor— kind, mild-mannered Victor—kept surfacing, demanding justice.

Sam's voice was steady, despite the flutter of nerves in her stomach. "I hear you, Beau. I do. But I can't just let Rosalita intimidate me into silence. Victor was our friend. He deserves better than to simply vanish without a trace. And if Rosalita thinks she can scare me off with legal threats, well …" Sam's lips curved into a smile. "She clearly doesn't know who she's dealing with."

"Sam, honey, I understand how you feel, but—"

"No buts," Sam interrupted, her voice firm. "I'll be careful, I promise. But I won't back down. Not when there's so much at stake."

Beau's eyes, warm with affection, met Sam's. "I know that look, sweetheart. There's no talking you out of this, is there?"

Sam reached out, gently squeezing his hand. "You know me too well," she said softly. "But I need you to trust me on this, Beau. I can handle it."

Beau's touch felt both comforting and conflicted. "I do trust you, Sam. It's everyone else I'm worried about. This investigation … it's stirring up trouble. And as much as I want to see justice for Victor, I can't bear the idea of you getting hurt."

Sam felt her emotions softening slightly at the genuine caring in his voice. "I know, honey. But I've faced worse than Rosalita's lawyer. Remember the Garrison case?"

A reluctant smile tugged at Beau's lips. "How could I forget? You nearly gave me a heart attack."

"And yet, here we are," Sam said, her tone lightening. "I promise to be extra careful this time. No midnight stakeouts or confrontations in dark buildings."

Beau's thumb traced circles on the back of her hand, his touch a silent plea. "Just … promise me you'll keep me in the loop? No going off on your own without backup?"

"I promise," Sam said solemnly, meeting his gaze as she stood up. She folded the loathsome piece of paper and jammed it into the pocket of her slacks.

He rose to his feet and they started back toward Sweet's Sweets.

During the walk back, both were quiet, Sam's mind filled with scenarios, both thrilling and terrifying. She pictured Sweet's Sweets, the business she'd built from the ground up, its reputation now at risk. She imagined the whispers of the townspeople, the sidelong glances, the potential loss of customers if she became involved in a nasty legal battle. She had friends and allies in this town—but so did Rosalita.

Then there was Beau, steadfast and loving, but caught between his duty as sheriff and his role as her husband. They reached the bakery parking lot and stopped beside his cruiser.

Sam managed a weak smile. "What if I'm the only one who can solve this? What if staying quiet means letting her get away with stealing everything Victor built—maybe even letting a killer walk free?"

Beau sighed, touching her chin and tipping her head up, bestowing a gentle kiss. "Just … be careful, okay? Don't take any unnecessary risks."

"I will," she promised, watching him slide into the vehicle and start it. With a quiet sigh, she stepped back into her bustling little business.

But her mind wouldn't settle on her work. Becky watched, sideways, as Sam picked up order sheets and then set them down, picked up decorating tools and dropped them.

"You need a break, boss. Listen, we've got this. It's just the normal afternoon crowd, and they'll soon be leaving. Why don't you go on home?"

Home. So she could pace the floor and stress herself endlessly over this situation? What she wanted right now was tea and comfort, and she knew just where to get them.

Sam bagged up an assortment of pastries and grabbed her keys, still distracted as she drove down Kit Carson Road. The adobe buildings seemed to glow in the late afternoon light, but their warmth did little to ease the knot in her stomach.

Seven minutes later, she pulled up to Zoë's B&B, a charming two-story house with a wrap-around porch. Sam found her friend in the kitchen, the scent of herbal tea already wafting through the air.

"Oh honey, you look like you've seen a ghost," Zoë said, pulling Sam into a quick hug before ushering her to the kitchen table.

Sam sank into a chair, placing the bag of pastries between them. "I might as well have," she sighed. "Zoë, I'm in over my head."

As Zoë poured tea into mismatched mugs, Sam recounted the events of the day—the discovery of the body that wasn't Victor, Rosalita's changing stories, and now the legal threat looming over her.

"I assured Beau I could handle this, but truthfully I don't know what to do," Sam concluded, wrapping her hands around the warm mug. "If I keep digging, I could lose everything. But if I don't …" Her voice trailed off.

Zoë pushed her long hair back, over her shoulder. "Sam, you remember how Victor fixed my garden fence last fall? He wouldn't take a dime for it, said it was just what neighbors do." Her eyes grew misty. "That man was as kind as they come. He deserves justice."

Sam nodded, feeling a lump form in her throat. "I know. But Rosalita's lawyer—"

"Rosalita," Zoë interrupted, her voice hardening slightly. "That woman gives me the creeps. Always has." She paused, considering her next words carefully. "Look, Sam, you have a gift. I admit, I don't fully understand how you to it, but you've solved mysteries before."

Sam tensed, still uncomfortable discussing her paranormal talents. "Maybe. But this feels different. Bigger."

Zoë reached across the table, clasping Sam's hand. "If anyone can get to the bottom of this, it's you."

"You're right," she said softly, meeting Zoë's gaze. "I can't let Rosalita or her lawyer scare me off. Not when there's so much at stake."

Chapter 19

Sam's hand was on Zoë's kitchen doorknob when her friend's voice called out behind her.

"Wait, Sam! I just remembered something that might help."

Sam turned, eyebrows raised in curiosity. "Okay …"

"Victor left some of his tools here last autumn," Zoë explained. "They're in the garden shed. Want to take a look?"

Sam smiled, remembering the toolbox she'd found in her own place. The man, although organized in so many ways, was completely scattered in others. "Absolutely. Let's take a look."

Zoë led the way. Sam's mind grasped for ideas. At this point, she'd take anything that came along.

"I've been meaning to return them," Zoë said softly, her

loose skirt swishing as they walked. "But with everything going on at the B&B …"

"Don't worry about it," Sam reassured her. "I'm just glad you remembered."

The sound of their footsteps on the pathway somehow reminded Sam of her childhood in Texas. Zoë reached for the shed door, and it creaked open. The interior was cluttered with gardening equipment, and a faint scent of earth and oil wafted out.

"Wow," Sam muttered, taking in the chaos. "Finding anything in here might be like looking for a needle in a haystack made of needles."

Zoë chuckled nervously. "Darryl's been meaning to organize it. You know how contractors are—always too busy with other people's projects to tackle their own."

Sam really wished she'd handled the wooden box earlier on this day. So many new facts, so many things to sort through. She waited as Zoë scanned the cluttered shelves. When her friend pointed to a sturdy plastic caddy filled with garden tools, sitting on a wooden shelf near the back, Sam reached for it.

"I'm pretty sure this is it," Zoë said, as Sam carefully lifted it down. She grunted softly as she set it on the ground.

"Glad I spotted it," Zoë exclaimed. "I wasn't even sure where Darryl had put it."

Sam knelt beside the caddy. "Let's see what we've got here." She began to pick through the items. The assortment of tools was neatly arranged, each in its designated spot. It was so orderly, so typically Victor, that Sam felt another pang of nostalgia for her missing friend.

As her eyes swept over the contents, something unusual caught her attention. Tucked beside a trowel was a small, leather-bound notebook. Sam reached for it, puzzled.

"What's that?" Zoë asked, peering over Sam's shoulder.

Sam held the notebook gingerly. "I'm not sure," she replied, her voice barely above a whisper. "But something tells me it might be important." *Like maybe the client list and schedule I'll probably never get from Rosalita now.*

Sam carefully opened the notebook, its worn cover creaking slightly. The first page revealed Victor's familiar handwriting, the slightly slanted script immediately recognizable. But as she began to read, her eyes widened.

"Well, it's not a schedule," Sam breathed, her eyebrows rising.

Zoë bent in closer to see. "What is it, Sam?"

"It's Victor's writing, but … it's strange. Cryptic, almost." Sam ran her finger down the page. "Listen to this: 'The shadow grows longer. Too close to home now. Must be careful.'"

Zoë's warm brown eyes met Sam's. "That sounds … weird, a little ominous. What do you think it means?"

Sam shook her head, holding the book to the sunlight filtering through the shed's dusty window. "I'm not sure, but it doesn't sound good. There's more here about a threat, but it's all so vague."

As Sam continued to read, her frown deepened. "Zoë, this talks about someone 'too close to home' and hints at some kind of danger Victor felt was looming over him."

Zoë's usual serene expression gave way to concern. "Oh, Sam. Too close to home … sounds like Rosalita."

Sam nodded slowly, her gut feeling aligning with Zoë's suggestion. "Yeah. We all knew they had their issues, and now this …" She gestured at the notebook, "This suggests something much more serious, an actual threat."

"Zoë!" Darryl's voice called out from the B&B. "Phone call!"

Zoë touched Sam's arm. "I'd better go. Stay as long as you want."

Sam nodded, her expression grim. "Okay, thanks. Go on, I'll study this a bit more before I leave."

As Zoë's footsteps faded, Sam turned the notebook over. Three small slips of paper slipped loose. Receipts of some kind, she noticed, tucking them into the back of the book.

Turning the pages, each filled with more of Victor's fragmented ideas and hurried sketches, Sam's pulse quickened. The urgency in his writing came through, even though it read more like poetic sayings. She suddenly remembered Novelle Rojas talking about Victor having a creative side, how he wrote little verses. Perhaps it was just that—poetry or fiction.

She paused at a page with a rough sketch of what looked like a tree, its branches twisted unnaturally. Beside it, Victor had scrawled, "*El árbol sabe - pero no puede hablar.*" Pretty straightforward—the tree knows, but cannot speak.

"What in the world does that mean? Is it a clue to something that was actually going on in his life, or just an imaginary reference to a tree that caught his fancy?"

"Hey, Sam." The familiar male voice startled her so abruptly that she shrieked and dropped the notebook.

"Darryl, I hereby hold you responsible for the heart attack I'm about to have," she said with a laugh.

"Sorry. Didn't mean to scare you. Zoë asked if you were hungry and want to stay for supper."

"Thanks, but no. I need to get going soon. Beau's had a long day and we'll just want to settle in."

"She said you're looking through Victor's things, trying to figure out where he went?"

"Yeah, and it's a challenge. I get the feeling he was disturbed about something, maybe frightened …"

Darryl gave a thoughtful nod. "I don't know about the handyman or gardening aspects of it, but I'll tell you, as a builder I'm feeling the pressure to scale up. And I really don't want to. I'm getting too old to battle it out in a young man's game. Let the Tommy Barkers and his generation take over, as far as I'm concerned."

"Really? You're thinking of retiring?"

"Don't sound so surprised, Sam. I'm older than you are. I guess it's just after a winter of dealing with muscle aches every single day …"

"I know what you're saying. I met Tommy Barker recently. So, he's the new guy in the game, huh?"

"Seems like. I've known him a few years now, but it's just recently he seems to have some new ideas about cornering the trade, hiring my crews away from me, big plans to offer full-package deals on new construction." He gave a shrug. "Who knows … maybe I'm reading more into it because I'm feeling my age. Ignore me."

He gave her a pat on the shoulder and headed back toward the house. Sam realized she really should get going. She set Victor's tool caddy aside, keeping the notebook so she could go through it later.

The scent of onions and beef greeted her when she walked through the front door at home.

"Hey, you timed it perfectly," Beau called out from the kitchen. "I was just about to call you. Two of our favorites from Lota Burger are ready!"

She laughed, appreciating his sensitivity for when she

loved the task of cooking and when it was not even on her radar. They carried their burgers and fries to the living room where they sat on comfy chairs and watched a game show, rather than discussing their difficult day and all the worries. Another thing she loved about this man.

"Since you did the cooking, I'll handle the cleanup," she said, wadding the wrappers and stuffing them into the bag.

"And I shall have a shower and probably do nothing. I've already got Danny taking care of the horses, so I'll most likely declare an early bedtime."

"Go for it." Sam carried the trash to the kitchen waste can and put the kettle on for a cup of tea. Her eyes landed on Victor's notebook, which she'd laid on the table when she arrived.

Tiptoeing upstairs, she found the carved box on her dresser top and picked it up. As always, the wood warmed to her touch and began to glow with a lovely golden color. She carried it down to the kitchen, poured boiling water into a mug, and held the box on her lap while her tea steeped.

The tingle in her hands told her she was ready to investigate. Carrying notebook, mug, and box to the living room, she settled into her favorite corner of the sofa. She set the box aside and opened the notebook. The small slips of paper fell out again, and she took a moment to study them. Grocery store receipt, post office receipt, and one from a self-storage unit. The name seemed familiar, but she didn't take the time to figure it out as she placed the notebook flat on her lap.

"Okay," she whispered to herself, "let's see what we can see."

Closing her eyes, Sam focused intently on the feel of the notebook in her hands. She concentrated, hoping for a glimpse of Victor's aura or perhaps his fingerprints—anything that might give her more insight into his state of mind when he wrote these unsettling notes.

"Come on, Victor," she muttered, her eyes still closed. "Show me something. Anything."

Sam opened her eyes; a faint shimmer caught her attention. A gossamer-thin outline of golden light traced the edges of the notebook, pulsing gently. She blinked, focusing harder, and the aura intensified. Flashes of deep red and murky green swirled within the gold, creating a turbulent pattern that made her stomach clench.

"*Dios mío*," Sam breathed, unconsciously echoing one of Victor's favorite phrases. The anxiety and fear radiating from the notebook were almost tangible. "What had you so scared, Victor?"

She turned the book over in her hands, watching the aura move and dance. The red seemed to pool around certain pages, as if Victor's fear had been particularly intense when writing those entries. Was he worried about his health, as Rosalita had implied?

"Okay, Sam," she said to herself, squinting at the fireplace. "Think this through. What do we know, and what do we need to find out?"

So many possibilities. Victor's cryptic notes, his apparent fear, his sudden disappearance—it all pointed to something far more sinister than a simple case of a man skipping town. But what? And how was she going to unravel this thing without putting herself, or others, in danger?

She again glanced down at the notebook in her hands,

its worn leather cover a stark reminder of the gravity of her discovery. Her first instinct was to tell Beau, to share this potentially crucial piece of evidence with her husband. But as she looked toward the top of the stairs, she hesitated.

"Damn it," she muttered. "This is exactly the kind of thing that puts Beau in a tough spot."

He'd been forced to serve her with a legal document this afternoon. Putting him in the middle of her investigation, sharing Victor's personal notes at this stage …

Sam sighed, holding onto the edges of the notebook. "If I bring this to him now, he'll have to act on it officially. But if I don't …"

She trailed off, her conscience warring with common sense. After a moment, she made her decision.

"Kelly," she said firmly, nodding to herself. "The next time I see her, we'll work on this. Once I tell her about the images on these pages, she'll understand the paranormal angle, and we can figure out our next move together."

Meanwhile, she sat with the book open on her lap, flipping pages. "'Too close to home,'" she muttered, remembering one of Victor's more unsettling phrases. "And deception—what did you mean by that, Victor? And why couldn't you just come out and say it?" That word had come up in one of their readings in the book of runes.

The night air had turned chilly, and Sam got up to close the window at the back of the house. As she made the rounds, checking locks, she realized that suddenly the day's stresses were piling up on her. She saw to it that the dogs had clean water and were now curled up on their beds near the fireplace, then she carried the book and box upstairs. Beau was sound asleep already.

It wasn't until she finished her bedtime preparations

and was reaching to switch off the lamp, that she realized something: the receipt from the self-storage unit was the second one she'd found from the same place. This was an ongoing rental. But before she could give any thought to the significance of that, her eyes closed and she drifted away.

Chapter 20

Sam woke with a start, rolling over to see the numerals on the clock—4:21. Ugh. Well, what did she expect? She and Beau had both been exhausted and had gone to bed super early. He was still asleep, but she knew he would be up soon. Ranch chores, breakfast, and appearing at his office in time for the seven a.m. briefing.

She slipped out of bed and pulled on warm sweats. Downstairs, she opened Victor's notebook again. The aura and mystical gold thread were gone now, but the receipts remained—she needed to figure out if they held any significance. She carried the leatherbound book to the kitchen, turning to the last page of it while the coffee brewed.

Victor's last entry caught her eye: An offer I don't like. *No quiero hacerlo.*

Sam squinted. She thought it meant he didn't want to do *it*—do something … She wasn't sure.

On the next-to-last page, most of the entries were written entirely in Spanish, but a name stood out. Talia Simpson.

"The real estate lady?" Sam walked to the counter and poured coffee into her favorite mug.

She recalled her visit to Talia's office, how the woman had seemed unhappy with Victor's work and then ranted about Rosalita's interference. Could it be that his notes in the book related to that? She could stop by Beau's office and ask Rico to translate, but she remembered the new homicide case. The deputies would be busy.

She could probably find an online translator of some kind, but maybe she should just pop in on Talia Simpson again and see what reaction she got. The woman might be able to shed more light on Victor's current situation. And this time she would handle the wooden box before she met with the woman. As she drove into town, she concocted her cover story.

The receptionist's desk was unoccupied when Sam arrived, a little after nine. Her eyes swept across the room, taking in the vibrant Southwestern artwork adorning the walls and the sleek modern furniture that seemed at odds with the traditional architecture.

A faint aroma of coffee wafted from another room, mingling with the scents of new carpeting and printer toner. Sam followed the path she'd taken before, down the corridor to the boss's office.

She tapped on the door's edge and called out. "Ms. Simpson? Sorry to interrupt. There was no one out front."

Talia looked up, startled, her wild, pale blonde curls seemed to defy gravity, framing a face that bore the lines of stress and over-tanning. Her workspace was still a whirlwind of papers and colorful sticky notes surrounding an ornate metal lamp.

"Ah, yes, Samantha. I don't have a lot of time this morning." Multiple bracelets clinked as the woman shuffled papers. "I've got three closings this afternoon and the damn paperwork—" She glanced up. "Sorry. This county doesn't make things simple, do they? I mean, back in Florida where I started my career … Never mind. What can I help you with?"

Sam's gaze lingered on the silver and turquoise jewelry, automatically cataloging the craftsmanship. But it was the erratic flashes in Talia's aura that truly captured Sam's focus. Chaotic bursts of muddy orange pulsed around her, a clear sign of some kind of underlying tension, maybe deceit.

Sam snapped herself back to the present. "Would you have a minute to chat about the charming adobe in the three-hundred block of Pueblo Road?" She'd picked up that address from a scribbled notation inside the back cover of Victor's notebook.

Talia's head snapped up, her saleswoman smile automatic. "Of course, of course," she said, gesturing to a chair. "That was built by one of the area's best contractors. Please, have a seat. Always happy to discuss our properties."

Sam couldn't help but notice that, despite her smile, Talia's aura flared, murky now. Interesting, Sam thought. Very interesting indeed.

Sam kept her tone casual. "I heard there were some recent renovations on that property. Victor Martinez was involved, wasn't he? I've always felt his work is top-notch."

Talia's forced smile faltered, replaced by a tightness around her eyes. The aura swirled.

"Victor." Talia's voice held a sharp edge. "Yes, well, he was *supposed* to handle some repairs, but … Well, we've had to put a hold on the listing because the home is not ready to show."

Sam's eyebrows raised slightly. "Oh? Was there a problem with the work?"

Talia's gaze darted away, focusing on the papers before her. "Let's just say the job wasn't completed to our satisfaction, and I am *not* working with that woman of his," she muttered, shuffling the documents with unnecessary force.

Rosalita, Sam thought, watching the aura pulse red, on the verge of anger. She remembered Talia's previous comments about the ex-wife and put on a sympathetic expression. "That must have been frustrating. Did Victor explain why he couldn't finish or give any idea when he would return?"

Talia shrugged it off. "Nothing. But we'll find someone else. Someone who shares our vision."

Sam considered. Maybe that's what Victor's notation meant—he didn't like working with this particular customer. Maybe her offer was way too low for the amount of work she wanted him to do. It may have had nothing to do with his reasons for leaving town.

Talia's manicured hands waved dramatically, her turquoise rings catching the light. "Honestly, it's all Victor's fault we can't show that particular home," she said. "If he'd just done his job …"

Sam kept her expression neutral. *Let her talk.*

"I mean, really," Talia went on, her voice rising slightly. "How hard is it to show up and finish what you started? We've had to scramble to find other repairmen and landscapers, and it's cost us a fortune."

"So, you haven't been able to reach Victor at all?"

Talia's aura again flashed a deep, angry red. "No," she snapped. "As I told you the other day. And frankly, I don't care to. As far as I'm concerned, he can stay disappeared."

Sam refused to react to that statement. "You know, I couldn't help but notice you have listings on quite a few high-dollar homes, more expensive than average for this area."

Talia's smile brightened, the corners of her mouth twitching. "The market's been good to us," she said, simply. "Taos is becoming quite the hot spot. Now, if there's nothing else—"

"Actually," Sam interjected gently, "I was hoping we could circle back to that property on Pueblo Road. The one Victor was working on before he left."

Talia did an impatient exhale. "What about it?"

"I'm just trying to put together the timeline," Sam pressed, keeping her tone light. "When exactly did the work stop? And was there some kind of argument before Victor disappeared?"

"I've told you everything I know," Talia insisted, her voice rising. "Sometime in December, Victor left us high and dry, end of story. I don't know why you're so interested, but I can assure you, I had nothing to do with his vanishing act!"

Sam raised an eyebrow, maintaining her calm demeanor even as her suspicions solidified. "I never suggested you did, Talia," she said softly, watching for any telltale twitches.

"I've told you everything," she repeated. Standing up, she dabbed at moisture forming at her temple. "Thank you for the brownies the other day, but now if you'll excuse me,

I have someone waiting."

Sam rose as well, offering a polite nod. "Of course," she said smoothly. "Thank you for your time, Talia. Take care."

Talia knew far more than she was letting on. The defensive posture, her erratic responses, and that flickering aura all pointed to a woman with something to hide. But what exactly was Talia Simpson concealing? Her emotional state seemed a lot more complex than some unfinished jobs warranted.

Sam strode past the reception desk, then stopped in her tracks. Sitting in the waiting room was Tommy Barker. He looked up, offering only a tight smile before shifting his attention back to his phone screen. The receptionist was saying something into the phone receiver, then she looked up and told Tommy he could go on back.

Sam pushed through the door to the street, letting out a long breath. The bustling sounds of the real estate office faded, replaced by the hum of traffic on the plaza. She got into her van and started it, mentally cataloging the clues from their encounter.

"Well, that was … illuminating," she muttered to herself. Maybe Tommy Barker was the contractor Talia was paying to do repairs on the homes, which could make sense.

Considering the entry in Victor's notebook and the conversation just now, Talia Simpson was involved in this thing, one way or another. Maybe it would help if Sam could find out more about Talia's financial situation. Was she making a killing in the real estate market, or was that all for show?

"I'm going to figure it out, one clue at a time." A

pinch between her eyebrows signaled the beginning of a headache. "But right now, I need to go beat some cake batter or something."

Chapter 21

She walked in the back door at Sweet's Sweets six minutes later, ready to take her mind off the case for a while. Baking and decorating always took her into a world of sugar and spice and got her away from the worries that had plagued her sleep.

"Hey, Sam, you're just in time," Becky called out. "Someone came in and cleaned us out of cupcakes. The bunnies and chicks are completely gone."

Sam looked around, taking in the situation. Four dozen cupcakes were in the bake oven, and another three dozen sat on the cooling racks, awaiting icing and decorations. She donned her baker's jacket and washed her hands.

Filling pastry bags with white, yellow, and pink buttercream, she began covering the tops of the cupcakes, passing them over to Becky for the little details. Blobs of piped icing soon took the shape of bunnies, with delicate dots for eyes and whiskers. Becky switched out the white for some yellow, and cute chicks began to adorn nests of coconut.

Within the hour they had enough to replenish the display cases out front. Jen sent a grateful smile her way when Sam brought out the first two dozen.

"I was a little worried we'd have a rebellion on our hands," she said with a smile. "Two schools placed last-minute orders."

"Julio's got theirs out of the oven, into the cooler, and we're starting on the decorations next," Sam assured her. "What else is running low?"

"Lemon bars. We can't seem to keep enough today. Oh—and the raspberry tarts. Did you advertise those, or is it just word of mouth?"

"Gotta be word of mouth." As she said it, two ladies walked through the front door and pointed toward the case.

"I'll be right back," Sam murmured to Jen.

The walk-in fridge held about a dozen of the tarts, which they'd baked yesterday. She called out to Julio to get more started, while she carried the remaining inventory out to the front.

"Slightly crazy week," Becky said when Sam came back into the kitchen.

"No one's getting time for lunch breaks, are we?" Sam asked, surveying the lineup of work for the afternoon. "How about if I run out and pick up pizzas?"

Julio smiled, and Becky practically swooned. "That would be fabulous."

At eleven-thirty, she headed out.

Despite placing her order ahead of time, Sam was told it would be another fifteen minutes when she arrived at Taos Pizza Palace. But the warm scents of oregano and cheese enveloped her, and there was a happy ambiance of chatter in the crowded dining room. She took a seat in the lobby and decided to check her email.

When she heard heavy boots on the wooden floor, Sam's head snapped up from her phone, her eyes spotting Tommy Barker as he strode purposefully toward the counter. His long, dark braid hung down his back. More than one female in the place noticed the rigid set of his broad shoulders beneath his worn denim work shirt.

Sam tucked her phone away, glancing up at Tommy's face. His chiseled features were set in a scowl that seemed to dare anyone to approach him. She'd always found it ironic how someone so skilled at creating beautiful things with wood could have such a prickly demeanor.

"Large Coke and an order of breadsticks," Tommy demanded of the cashier, not bothering with pleasantries.

Sam cleared her throat. "Hi, Tommy. Fancy running into you twice in one day. How'd your meeting go with Talia?"

He grunted in response, barely sparing her a glance, but a flush crept up his neck and suddenly Sam knew— those two were an item. Sam resisted the urge to tease him about it.

Tommy collected his drink and took a long swig, settling into the chair next to Sam's, to wait for his breadsticks. "So, I hear Marcos Sanchez skipped town right after that body turned up in the arroyo. The sheriff say what that's about?"

Sam thought her mouth had fallen open. *Marcos, gone?*

"Course it ain't my business what that little punk does,"

Tommy muttered, but his tone lacked its usual edge. "And the body's not Victor, is it?"

Sam glanced around, noticing a few curious patrons trying to eavesdrop. "It's not. Listen, why don't we step over to that corner booth for a minute? I'd like to hear more."

Tommy's jaw clenched, and for a moment, Sam thought he might refuse. Then he gave a curt nod, grabbing his drink and following her to the secluded booth.

As they settled onto the cracked vinyl seats, Sam realized she needed to tread carefully here. Tommy's abrasive personality and his grudge against Victor made him a wildcard in this investigation. But if he knew something about Marcos's disappearance, it could provide valuable information.

"Look," Sam began, keeping her tone casual, "I'm just trying to piece together what happened with Victor. Marcos's sudden departure seems … odd, don't you think?"

Tommy sat back, crossing his muscular arms across his chest. "Like I said, not my problem. That kid's always been a pain."

Sam nodded. She'd seen Marcos's shiny new pickup truck, heard of his reputation with the girls. While he was whining about not having money, he sure was spending a lot. It was hard to believe he and the hardworking Victor were related.

"True," she agreed. "But leaving town right after a body is found? That's more than just trouble. That's suspicious. I wonder if he assumed the body was Victor and that he'd be questioned."

Tommy squeezed his drink cup, agitated. "Wouldn't surprise me. Maybe he just got scared. Or maybe he finally pissed off the wrong person. Who knows with that hothead?"

"Hothead. Did you see something before he left? Anything at all?"

For a long moment, Tommy said nothing, his dark eyes studying her face. Sam held his gaze, silently willing him to trust her. Finally, he sighed, uncrossing his arms.

"Look, Sam," he said, his voice gruff but lacking its usual hostility, "I might've seen something. But I ain't getting mixed up in this mess. You understand?"

"I understand," she said finally. She gave him a crooked smile. "But c'mon … What did you see?"

"Okay, yeah, I saw him and Rosalita going at it outside Walmart, a few days before he disappeared. Wasn't pretty."

"So, what happened?"

"This stays between us, got it?" Tommy's eyes took on a distant look, and she realized he was a born story teller.

"It was late afternoon, sun was real low in the sky," Tommy began, his voice low and gruff. "I was heading to my truck when I heard shouting. Turned around and there they were, right by the garden center."

Sam could almost see it herself: the long shadows across the Walmart parking lot, the scent of exhaust mingling with the aroma of newly watered plants.

Tommy continued, his words painting a vivid picture. "Marcos was all worked up, waving his arms around like some kinda crazy windmill. Face all red, veins popping in his neck. And Rosalita, she was just standing there with her arms crossed, cool as you please. Didn't raise her voice once, but man, if looks could kill …"

It hadn't occurred to her that Marcos's disappearance might not have been voluntary. Now it did. Sam tensed, imagining the scene. Marcos, young and volatile, facing off against his uncle's ex, a woman who could be as immovable as Taos Mountain when she wanted to be. "What were they arguing about?" Sam asked, her voice barely audible.

Tommy shrugged. "Couldn't make out everything, but I heard Marcos yelling about money and family loyalty. Rosalita, she just stood there with this look on her face. Like she knew something he didn't."

Sam would bet that much was true.

Tommy's eyes gleamed with contempt. "Marcos's face was redder than a sun-dried tomato. He jabbed his finger at Rosalita, spitting out words like they were poison. 'You've got no right to meddle in my family's affairs, you old *bruja*!'"

A sly grin spread across Tommy's face as he continued. "But Rosalita? She didn't even flinch. Just smiled at him, sweet as pie, but with these cold, cold eyes. She got close to him and whispered something I couldn't catch, but whatever it was, it shut Marcos up quick."

"Sounds like quite the showdown," Sam prodded, hoping to glean more information.

Tommy snorted, leaning back in his seat. "Yeah, well, serves the kid right. Always strutting around like he owns the place, just 'cause his uncle's got a successful business."

"Seems like you've got some strong feelings about Marcos and Rosalita?"

Tommy shrugged. "Ain't got nothin' to say about them," he muttered, but his dark eyes flickered with something Sam couldn't quite place. Resentment? Anger?

"Come on, Tommy," Sam pressed gently. "There's clearly some history there."

"Forget it. It don't matter now anyway."

Sam nodded slowly, piecing together what she knew

about Marcos. The image of the cocky young man, his arrogant smirk. "You know, I always wondered how Marcos managed to keep up with that flashy lifestyle of his. That truck of his couldn't have been cheap."

Tommy's eyes narrowed slightly. "Yeah, well, some people don't know how to live within their means. Look, Sam, I ain't one to gossip, but …" He glanced around, lowering his voice as he began to do just that. "Marcos was asking around for money before he split. Seemed pretty desperate, if you ask me."

Sam's eyebrows shot up. This was new information—his financial hounding going beyond his own uncle. "Really? Did he approach you?"

Tommy snorted. "As if I'd have anything to spare. Nah, but I heard him hitting up some of the guys at the construction site. Even tried his luck with old Mrs. Alvarez at the diner."

"And no one thought to mention this before?"

"People don't like to air other folks' dirty laundry," Tommy shrugged. "At least, not to the sheriff's wife."

That was the crux of it—Sam's relationship to the sheriff—which might account for the lack of progress when she asked questions around town. Now she had to wonder, was it just Marcos's reckless spending catching up with him, or was there something more sinister at play?

"Tommy," she said carefully, "do you think Marcos's money troubles have anything to do with his disappearance? Or Victor's, for that matter?"

The carpenter's face hardened. "I ain't saying nothing more, Sam. You start poking around too much, you might not like what you find."

With that cryptic warning, Tommy stood up abruptly,

his boots scraping against the wooden floor. He grabbed his order of breadsticks and headed for the door, leaving Sam to absorb all the new information.

Marcos gone. He and Rosalita in a huge argument a few days ago. Could Rosalita's conflicting stories be a cover for something more sinister?

"Order up for Sam! Large supreme, medium pepperoni and mushroom!" The pizza guy's voice barely registered until she blinked, suddenly aware of the bustling pizzeria around her.

"Oh, right. Thanks," she mumbled, retrieving her pizza boxes. She walked out to her van, the sunny day a contrast to her mood.

As she drove, the warm, savory pizza aroma wafted up, and Sam's attention jumped around. Marcos's cocky attitude and financial troubles, Rosalita's conflicting stories, Tommy's revelations—it all swirled together like a complex recipe she couldn't quite decipher.

"What's your play here, Rosalita?" she said aloud in the quiet of her van. "If I push too hard, she'll lawyer up faster than I can say 'obstruction of justice.' But if I don't dig deeper ..."

She sighed, picturing Beau's face. Her husband would caution her to be careful, to let the official investigation play out. But Sam knew, somehow, that time was running out.

Chapter 22

The pizza was a big hit, each of the Sweet's Sweets crew grabbing a slice and taking stools around the big worktable to eat. Jen carried hers away, keeping an eye on the sales counter the whole time.

"Ummm, this really hit the spot," Julio said, polishing off his second slice and going back to the huge Hobart mixer to stir up chocolate batter for three birthday cakes.

Sam cleared away the empty pizza boxes and the napkins, while Becky decorated more cookies, piping delicate frosting flowers onto each sugary canvas. Sam's mind, however, was far from the cheerful confections spread on the table as she pitched in to help with the rest of the cookies.

The interviews of the morning, plus the news of Victor's nephew, Marcos, now also disappearing, competed for mental space with the mounting orders for the upcoming holiday.

Sam sighed, setting down the piping bag and flexing her cramped hands. "I can't keep doing this," she said to herself, her voice barely audible over the hum of the refrigerator. "The bakery needs me here, not chasing down leads that go nowhere."

"What?" Becky asked. Having cleared the table of sugar cookies, she was carrying the final tier for a wedding cake from the fridge.

Sam shook her head and glanced at the clock, realizing with a start that she'd lost track of time again. The wedding cake for the Anderson-Baca nuptials was due in less than two hours. "Do you need a hand with that?"

Becky sent a smile in her direction. "Nope. I saved the easiest tier for last. If you could hand me that topper, the one with the yellow lilies ... Uh, Sam, those are pink. I need the yellow."

Get it together, Sam, she chided herself, handing Becky the correct piece. As she worked, her memories drifted to the recent string of mysteries she'd found herself embroiled in. Each one had pulled her away from Sweet's Sweets, leaving her staff to shoulder the burden of her absences.

The bells above the door tinkled, and Sam craned her neck to look toward the sales room. A young couple entered, their eyes wide as they took in the display cases filled with Easter-themed treats.

"Welcome to Sweet's Sweets," Jen's voice called out. "What can I get for you today?"

Reassured that Jen had the front room under control, a part of Sam's mind remained fixed on Victor and all the unanswered questions, even as she carried the newly decorated cookies out to the display case.

With the couple's order boxed and paid for, Jen moved over to the beverage bar to check the coffee supply. Sam paused, wiping a smudge of powdered sugar from her hands onto her apron, and found her gaze drawn to the window. Outside, the young couple drove away. She noticed two customers at Puppy Chic next door, one holding a fluffy white Maltese in her arms, the other walking inside to pick up a pet.

Sam's shoulders sagged. "Maybe it's time to step back," she murmured.

She closed her eyes, picturing Beau's tired face when he'd come home late last night, having lost track of time while following up on a potential lead about his new homicide case. "I can't keep doing this to him, to the bakery, to myself," she said softly.

The ding of the oven timer jolted her back to reality, and Sam moved back to the kitchen. The least she could do was check their supplies and place an order with her wholesaler. Could she really step away from the mysteries that seemed to find her? Or was her gift—and the responsibility that came with it—too integral a part of who she was now?

"One thing at a time, Sam," she told herself firmly, focusing on the task at hand.

She'd just completed her online order when she heard the back door open, and Sam looked up to see Kelly breeze in, her curly hair caught up in a messy bun. The familiar sight of her daughter brought an immediate sense of comfort, easing some of the tension Sam had been carrying.

"Hey, Mom!" Kelly called out cheerfully, her smile sparkling. "Whoa, Easter cookie central in here, huh?"

Sam managed a smile. "You know how it gets this time

of year. What brings you by?"

Kelly ran a hand over the smooth worktable as she studied her mother's face. "I finished my day at Puppy Chic and just thought I'd pop in. You okay? You look … I don't know, a little frazzled."

Sam sighed, shutting down her computer. "Is it that obvious?"

"Only to someone who knows you as well as I do," Kelly said softly. She reached out, touching Sam's arm. "Mom, when was the last time you took a break? And I mean a real break, not just five minutes between batches of cookies."

Sam's shoulders slumped. "I can't even remember," she admitted. "It's been a crazy day and I woke up shortly after four a.m."

Kelly's eyes lit up. "I've got an idea. Why don't you come over to the house later? We could have some tea, maybe do a little *reading*. It might help clear your head, give you some perspective." She meant the book of runes.

Sam hesitated. "I don't know, Kel. I've got this wedding cake to deliver, and—"

"And after that," Kelly interrupted gently, "you're coming over."

Sam found herself nodding. She remembered her questions about Victor's notebook, all the pages written in Spanish, and a small spark of hope ignited in her chest. Kelly's Spanish was far better than Sam's, and this might be the perfect chance to get it translated. "You're right. Okay, I'll come by after I drop off the cake. It might be good to step back and refocus."

Kelly beamed. "Perfect. I'll have everything ready. And Mom?" She squeezed Sam's hand. "Whatever's going on, we'll figure it out. That's what family's for, right?"

As Kelly left, Sam felt some of the burden lift from her shoulders. She might not have all the answers yet, but she wasn't alone in searching for them. And sometimes, that made all the difference.

Two hours later, Sam pulled up to Kelly's Victorian home, the late afternoon sun casting long shadows across the front lawn. Before she could even reach the porch, the front door flew open, and a blur of red hair and freckles came bounding out.

"Grammy!" Ana squealed, launching herself into Sam's arms. "You're just in time! Daddy's going to help me plan the most epic Easter egg hunt ever!"

Sam laughed, hugging her granddaughter tight. "Is that so? And where are you planning to hide all these eggs?"

Ana's eyes twinkled with mischief. "That's a secret. But I bet even you won't be able to find them all."

"Ana!" Scott's voice called from inside. "Time for your math lesson, sweetheart."

The little girl's nose scrunched up. "Do I have to? Grammy just got here."

Sam ruffled Ana's curls. "Go on, smarty-pants. Show those numbers who's boss. We'll catch up later, okay?"

As Ana reluctantly trudged inside, Sam couldn't help but marvel at her granddaughter's precociousness. At six years old—or "not quite two," as Ana liked to remind everyone because of her February twenty-ninth birthdate—she was already tackling subjects well beyond her years.

Kelly appeared in the doorway, a warm smile on her face. "Ready for our session, Mom?"

Sam nodded, following her daughter into the house. As they climbed the stairs to the attic, with Eliza the cat twining between them, she found herself wondering what insights the runes might offer this time. Would they shed any light on Victor's disappearance? Or perhaps offer some guidance on balancing her roles as baker and amateur sleuth?

The attic room was bathed in golden light as they entered, dust motes dancing in the air. Sam watched as Kelly moved, retrieving the carved wooden box and well-worn book of runes from a locked cupboard. Sam poured tea from the ceramic pot Kelly had carried up.

"I still can't believe how much this place has changed," Sam mused, settling into a chair at the worktable. "Remember when it was just full of cobwebs and old junk?"

Kelly chuckled, carefully placing the items between them. "Oh, I remember. It took weeks to clear and organize it. But now …" She gestured around the cozy space. "It's become our own little sanctuary."

As if on cue, Eliza sauntered past, leaping gracefully onto the sunny window seat. She fixed Sam with an inscrutable gaze, her tail swishing slowly.

"I swear that cat knows more than she lets on," Sam muttered, eyeing Eliza warily.

Kelly laughed. "Maybe she does. Ana certainly seems to think so." She paused, her expression growing more serious. "Speaking of which, have you noticed anything … unusual about Ana lately?"

Sam raised an eyebrow. "Unusual how?"

Before Kelly could respond, a muffled shriek of laughter drifted up from downstairs, followed by Scott's good-natured groan. Whatever Kelly had been about to say seemed to evaporate as she smiled fondly.

"Never mind," she said, reaching for the rune book. "Let's see what wisdom the ancients have for us today, shall we?"

Sam's attention was drawn to the carved lines on the wooden box. As Kelly opened the lid, a faint, earthy scent wafted out, carrying with it an air of ancient mysteries.

"It never fails to amaze me," Sam murmured, her earlier feelings of being overwhelmed fading as she focused on the task at hand. "How something so small can hold so much power."

Kelly nodded, carefully opening the book of runes. Each emblem on the page gleamed softly in the attic's warm light, their symbols seeming to shimmer as Sam's gaze moved over them.

"Ready?" Kelly asked, her voice barely above a whisper.

Sam felt a familiar tingle of anticipation.

They locked eyes across the table, and in that moment, Sam felt a surge of warmth and connection. Despite the years and the changes in their lives, this bond with her daughter remained unshakeable. It was more than just shared blood; it was a shared understanding of the many things they'd faced together.

"You know," Sam said, a wry smile tugging at her lips, "if someone had told me a few years ago that I'd be sitting in an attic, reading runes with my daughter, I'd have thought they were crazy."

Kelly laughed softly. "Life has a way of surprising us, doesn't it? But I wouldn't change it for the world."

Sam nodded, feeling a swell of pride and love for her daughter. She reached out to squeeze Kelly's hand. "You're so right. Now, let's see what we can learn."

Sam centered herself as she ran a hand over the spine

of the book. The soft breathing of the two women filled the attic room, mixing with the contented purr of Eliza on the window seat. Sam held the book upright, its spine resting on the table between her and Kelly.

"Ready?" Sam asked, releasing the two covers of the book so that it fell open to a random page.

Kelly nodded, leaning forward slightly.

Sam stared at the page until one of the runic symbols stood out. Her eyes followed the etched symbol. "Othala," she murmured, consulting the book. "It represents inheritance, ancestral property." She paused, considering. "It's about what we pass down through generations—not just possessions, but values, traditions."

Kelly's eyes widened. "That's ... surprisingly fitting, given our situation."

Sam couldn't help but agree. Their shared abilities, the very runes they were reading—all of it was a kind of inheritance, passed down through their family line. And Victor ... his home was an ancestral one.

"Mannaz," Sam said, her voice soft with wonder as she examined the second rune. "The self, the individual. But also humanity as a whole." She glanced up at Kelly. "It's about our connections to others, our place in the community." Which also fit Victor, exactly.

Kelly nodded slowly, her curly hair catching the afternoon light. "And the third?"

Sam's hand smoothed the page as she revealed the final rune. "Ehwaz," she breathed. "Partnership, trust." She looked up, meeting Kelly's gaze. "It's often associated with the bond between horse and rider, but it can represent any deep, trusting relationship."

"Such as Victor's relationship with all of us."

The significance wasn't lost on either of them. Sam felt a lump forming in her throat as she considered the implications. "Kelly," she said, her voice thick, "these particular runes, just revealed … they're all about family bonds. The inheritance we share, our individual roles, and the trust between us."

Kelly reached across the table, grasping Sam's hand. "It's like they're reminding us of what's really important," she said softly. "With everything going on—the bakery, the mysteries, Beau being back at his old job—maybe we needed this reminder of our foundation."

Sam nodded, feeling a wave of clarity wash over her. The overwhelm that had plagued her earlier seemed to dissipate in the face of this simple, profound truth. Whatever challenges lay ahead, she had this—this unbreakable bond with her daughter, with her family.

"You're right," Sam said, squeezing Kelly's hand. "We've got this."

Sam's gaze drifted to the attic window. The deep blue Taos sky stretched endlessly, reminding her of the vastness of life and the precious connections that anchored her within it. Her thoughts wandered to Beau, imagining him in his khaki sheriff's uniform, dealing with a homicide case and probably some other small-town dramas at the same time.

"You know," Sam said, her voice soft with reflection, "these runes make me think of Beau and our life here. How we've built something so … solid."

Kelly nodded, a knowing smile playing on her lips. "Beau has been your rock through all this sleuthing and through starting your bakery business, hasn't he?"

Sam chuckled. "Oh, more than he knows. Sometimes

I wonder how he puts up with all the chaos I drag home."

"Because he loves you, Mom," Kelly said simply. "And let's face it, Taos would be a lot less interesting without your skills and insights."

Sam raised an eyebrow. "You mean without *our* insights," she corrected, gesturing between them. "These family bonds the runes are talking about? They're what make us strong enough to face whatever comes our way."

Kelly's expression piqued with curiosity. "Speaking of which, do you think the runes are trying to tell us something specific about Victor's disappearance?"

Sam paused, considering. "I'm not sure," she admitted. "But maybe they're reminding us to look at the case through the lens of relationships. Who was close to Victor—Rosalita and Marcos. I still have to believe one or both of them know more about his disappearance than they're saying.

"Who might have had reason to want him gone?" Kelly posed the question, but Sam shrugged.

"I'm still trying to figure that out, but it could easily be one of those two." She turned and pulled Victor's small leatherbound notebook from her bag. "I've been wanting to show this to you, Kel. A lot of it is written in Spanish, which isn't my strong suit. Can you translate?"

Kelly opened the book to the pages Sam indicated, the latter entries in the book.

"Family secrets—I comprehend that one," Kelly mused. "They can be powerful motivators."

Sam nodded. "You're right. And maybe that's where we need to focus our attention next."

"If I can keep this overnight, I'll try reading it this evening after Ana goes to bed. Or I'll get out my translator app," she said with a wink.

Sam stood up. "Kelly, you know, I was seriously considering stepping back from this whole investigation. But now …" She shook her head, her eyes bright. "Now I feel like I can tackle it head-on."

"That's the Samantha Sweet I know," Kelly said with a grin.

Sam nodded, watching as Kelly locked the box and book away in the cupboard. "A team," she agreed. "And speaking of teams, I should probably check in with Beau. I haven't talked with him all day. Maybe he's made progress with his workload."

"Workload or not, solved mystery or not, you're both coming for Easter dinner, right?"

"Absolutely. Ana has already described exactly what she wants the dessert to be. Hint: it's coming from the bakery."

Kelly led the way downstairs, unable to stop laughing. In the kitchen, Sam deposited their tea cups in the sink and called out a goodbye to Ana and Scott. Now, if only she could put the clues together to figure out this confounding case.

Chapter 23

Sam thought about the deeper messages in the runes, all the way home. If they were significant to Victor's case, she could only think it pertained to Rosalita and Marcos. They were the only family Victor had nearby. She drummed her thumbs on the steering wheel, considering her options for how to proceed. Short of ripping into the floorboards and walls, Victor's house had already been searched, leaving few stones unturned. But Marcos … there was still a thread to pull there.

She glanced at the dashboard clock, realizing Beau wouldn't be home for at least another hour or two. Maybe a quick little detour …

Less than ten minutes later, she was at the Los Pinos Apartments, tapping on the manager's door.

A gruff-looking man in sweatpants and a sleeveless

undershirt answered. "What can I do for you?"

"Hi there," Sam said, injecting warmth into her tone. "I'm looking for some information on Marcos Sanchez. I understand he's a tenant?"

The manager grunted. "He'd better be. Owes this month's rent. But I haven't seen him around in several days now."

"So, you think he's moved out?"

A shrug. "He did mention renting a storage unit. Said he needed somewhere to keep his uncle's stuff."

Sam's pulse quickened. "You wouldn't happen to know which storage facility, would you?"

"Pretty sure it was that place over on Paseo del Pueblo Norte. Something like U-Store It, I think."

A smile tugged at Sam's lips. "Perfect. Thank you so much for your help."

She knew the place. Her buddy Rupert owned the facility. This was the break she needed.

Sam dialed Rupert's number, her foot tapping an impatient rhythm as it rang.

"Samantha, darling!" Rupert's exuberant voice filled the line. "To what do I owe the pleasure?"

"Rupe, I need a favor," Sam said, cutting to the chase. "I'm working a case, and I've got a lead. Marcos Sanchez rented a unit at your storage facility."

"I'll take your word for it. Do you know the unit number?"

"Oh, gosh …" Then something clicked. Those receipts! "One second …" She fished a hand into the depths of her bag and came up with the stray slip of paper. "I think it's number 237. And it's probably rented by Marcos's uncle, Victor Martinez. Is there any chance we could take a look inside?"

There was a pause on the other end. "Well, that's not exactly standard procedure, Sam," Rupert said, his tone hesitant. "But for you … I heard you were looking into Victor's disappearance, so I suppose we could make an exception. When did you want to go over? I'd need to meet you there."

"How about now?"

Twenty minutes later, Sam stood beside Rupert in front of the storage facility. The afternoon sun angled down on the rows of identical metal doors, their orange paint peeling slightly in the dry air.

Rupert fidgeted with the hem of his flowing purple tunic. "Looks like the place could use some maintenance. It's the kind of thing I'd hire Victor to do."

Sam nodded. "Exactly. And checking inside might help us find him."

She squared her shoulders. "Ready?" she asked, meeting Rupert's gaze.

He gave a small nod, handing her a small key. "I suppose. You and your secret missions, Sam. As a property owner, I'm not keen, but as a novelist I have to say you do keep me entertained."

Sam paused in front of the storage unit, her hand hovering over the lock. She exhaled, bracing herself for whatever lay beyond. "Here goes nothing," she muttered, sliding the key into place.

With a metallic groan, the door rolled up, the sound echoing. Sam blinked, adjusting to the dim interior. At least, thank goodness, nothing smelled dead.

"*Dios mío,*" she whispered, unconsciously echoing Victor's favorite expression.

The storage unit was a study in organized chaos. Neatly

stacked boxes lined one wall, their labels written in Victor's precise handwriting. Against the opposite wall stood a sturdy workbench, its surface covered in an array of tools and scattered papers.

"Well, this is certainly … eclectic," Rupert remarked, peering over Sam's shoulder.

Sam stepped inside, her eyes darting from object to object. "Most of this looks like Victor's stuff. His toolbox, those gardening supplies … Wait a second."

Her gaze landed on a corner of the unit where a sleek mountain bike stood against the wall. Next to it sat a duffel bag and a pile of clothes that looked far too trendy for Victor's taste.

"I'd bet my last churro that those belong to Marcos," Sam said, gesturing to the items. "Looks like Victor was letting him store some things here after all."

Rupert nodded. "Makes sense. That boy's always been short on space and long on stuff he can't afford."

Sam touched the edge of the workbench. "Something doesn't add up, Rupe. If Victor intended to move away, why would he leave all this behind? And why would Marcos take off now, just as we're asking questions?"

"Maybe these were things he didn't want to leave where Rosalita would go through them," Rupert answered with a shrug.

Or maybe it was more serious. She wasn't certain she wanted the answers to that.

Sam closed her eyes, focusing on the energy of the room. She got a feeling of … urgency. Like Victor left in a hurry, but he meant to come back. The latter gave her some measure of hope.

She opened her eyes and turned to Rupert. "We need

to go through everything here. There's got to be a clue somewhere that can tell us what happened to him."

Rupert nodded in agreement, his eyes scanning the cluttered space. Suddenly, he perked up, pointing to a shelf at the back of the unit. "Sam, darling, look over there. Is that a television set?"

Sam followed his gaze, her heart skipping a beat as she spotted the small TV with a built-in video player, and a box of videotapes beside it. "Good eye, Rupe," she said, making her way over to the shelf. She pulled the dusty cardboard box toward her, pulling out a home-recorded tape.

"Oh my," Rupert cooed, peering over her shoulder. "What do you think is on there? Telenovelas? Or perhaps some steamy home videos?" He wiggled his eyebrows suggestively.

Sam chuckled, despite the tension in her shoulders. "Let's hope not. But whatever it is, it's more likely to be a lead than that stack of rusted old shovels." She turned the tape over in her hands, but it wasn't labeled. Could this be the key to unraveling Victor's disappearance?

"I don't know, Rupe," she said, her voice barely above a whisper. "Watching this feels like an invasion of privacy. What if it's something personal?"

Rupert gave her a look. "Honey, you're trying to find a missing person. It's going to get personal."

Sam nodded slowly. "You're right. And if there's even a chance this could help us understand what happened to Victor, we have to take it." She clutched the tape tighter. "Let's see what secrets this little cassette holds."

Sam approached the small television set nestled among the clutter. Clearing a space and searching for an outlet, she plugged in the outdated device and inserted the tape. The whir of the VCR filled the storage unit, echoing off the concrete block walls.

"Moment of truth," she murmured, pressing play.

The screen flickered to life, static dancing across its surface before settling into a grainy image. Victor's familiar face came into focus, his expression serious.

"*Hola, amigos,*" Victor's voice crackled through the dusty speaker, his accent heavier than usual. "If you're watching this, then … *amiga,* things have not gone as planned."

"What's going on, Victor?" she whispered to the onscreen image.

Victor continued, his words a blend of English and Spanish. "I need to … *cómo se dice* … disappear for a while. It is not safe, you see. There are people, bad people, who want something from me."

He drew his calloused hands along the sides of his face. "*Dios mío,* I never meant for any of this to happen. But sometimes, life *tiene otros planes,* no?"

Yes, Sam thought, life often had other plans. She began to piece together the fragments of information. What had Victor stumbled upon? Who were these 'bad people' he mentioned?

"I have to protect my family," Victor's voice grew more urgent. "Rosalita, Marcos … they could be in danger too. That's why I had to go. But I leave this message, hoping that someone kind, someone smart like you, Samantha, might find it."

Sam's breath caught in her throat. He'd anticipated her involvement. But how? And then it hit her: by leaving the storage locker receipt in his toolbox at her bakery. Sooner or later she would find it.

"There is more to this story," Victor said, leaning

closer to the camera. "*Mucho más*. But I can't say it all here. Just know that the truth … it's hidden in plain sight. Look to the earth, where the seeds of the past grow into the present."

Sam's eyes widened, her pulse quickening as Victor's cryptic words sank in. She gripped the edge of the workbench, struggling to decipher his message. It was the type of poetic little phrase he used sometimes, the type of things he'd written in his various notebooks.

"The earth … seeds of the past," she muttered. Could he be referring to his gardening work? Or was it something more abstract?

Victor's face on the screen grew solemn. "Remember, Samantha, appearances can deceive. What looks like a rare flower might be a weed in disguise. Trust your *instintos*, your … special abilities."

Sam inhaled sharply. How did Victor know about her unique talents? She'd always been so careful to keep them under wraps.

"I'm sorry I cannot be more clear," Victor continued, his voice tinged with regret. "But if you're watching this, it means you are already on the right path. *Buena suerte*, my friend. And remember, sometimes the key to the future lies buried in the garden of the past."

The screen flickered, and Victor's image disappeared, leaving Sam standing in the dim light of the storage unit, her mind reeling.

"Garden of the past," she repeated softly. "Victor, what were you mixed up in?"

She turned to Rupert, her eyes blazing with renewed purpose. "We may need to check every property Victor worked on. Every garden, every flowerbed. There's something out there he wants us to find."

"Oh, girl, do you know what you're saying? That could take eons."

Sam reached out and switched off the television, leaving a silence in the storage unit that felt heavy, ripe with possibility. She inhaled the musty scent of cardboard boxes and old papers.

"Well, that was ... something," Rupert said, his voice sounding oddly loud in the quiet space.

"It certainly was. Victor's given us a lot to think about."

She turned, surveying the cluttered unit. The dim light cast long shadows across stacked boxes and forgotten trinkets. Each of them might hold potential significance. It was a little overwhelming.

"Rupert, I'm going to need some time here. There might be more clues hidden among Victor's belongings."

Rupert scratched his head. "Sure thing, Sam. Just ... be careful, all right? I don't want to get mixed up in anything too dicey."

Sam offered him a reassuring smile. "I'll be discreet." As Rupert left, closing the door behind him, Sam's smile faded.

"Okay, Victor," she murmured to the jam-packed room, "let's see what else you've left for me to find."

She approached the workbench, her eyes scanning the scattered tools and papers. Another video cassette, this one with a faded label caught her attention. As she reached for it, she felt a familiar tingle in her fingertips.

"Here we go," Sam whispered, bracing herself for whatever revelation might come next. She studied the label for some clue, ready to uncover the next piece of the puzzle that Victor had so carefully laid out for her.

Chapter 24

Sam's heart clenched as she carried the second videotape over to the player. Dust motes danced in the harsh overhead fluorescent light as she inserted the tape into the VCR. Again, Victor's face filled the screen, his usually immaculate appearance now disheveled. Dark circles shadowed his eyes, and his salt-and-pepper hair stood on end as if he'd been running his fingers through it repeatedly.

"*Hola, mi amiga*," Victor began, his voice hesitant. "I hope this tape finds you well. *Ay, dios mío*, where to begin?"

Sam moved closer, noting how this Victor seemed more uncertain than the one she'd watched in the previous recording. This must have been filmed later, she realized.

Victor cleared his throat, switching to English. "I have … how you say … stumbled upon something. Something big, *algo peligroso*." He glanced nervously over his shoulder, as if expecting someone to burst through the door at any moment.

Danger. What danger? Sam itched to jot down notes, but she didn't dare take her eyes off the screen. What had Victor discovered? And why did he look so afraid?

"I cannot say much, *no es seguro*," Victor continued. "But I must go away for a while. To protect … to protect those I care about."

"What are you mixed up in, Victor?" she murmured, wishing she could reach through the screen and shake answers out of him.

As if hearing her question, Victor's expression softened. "My friends, please trust that I do this for good reasons. When it is safe, I will return."

The tape ended abruptly, leaving Sam staring at a screen of static. She sat back, reeling. This recording raised more questions than it answered, but one thing was clear: Victor hadn't simply wandered off or gotten lost, and it didn't sound like he went away for medical care. He'd left deliberately, driven by some unknown threat.

"Oh, Victor, what mess have you gotten yourself into?"

She rewound the tape, deciding to watch it from the very beginning for any clues that might have come before. As Beau often said, the devil was in the details. And with Victor's life potentially on the line, she couldn't afford to overlook anything.

His face reappeared on the screen, his dark eyes filled with fear. "*Ay, Dios mío*," he muttered, running a hand through his graying hair. "I never thought it would come to this, *pero … la verdad …* the truth must be told."

His body tensed visibly. "*Rosalita, mi esposa …* she has been pushing, demanding money, signing papers. When I confront her ..." He trailed off, shaking his head.

This was it—the reason behind Victor's disappearance. But as she watched, Victor's expression darkened further.

"But that is not all," he continued, his voice dropping to a near-whisper. "There are people in this town, people who want big changes, some dangerous, some things I do not like. They are pushing, pushing me. They do not respect the land or the life." He swallowed hard, his eyes darting nervously off-screen.

Sam's mind whirled. People? Another suspect? Who could it be? Marcos? Someone else entirely? And what did Victor mean about Rosalita and Marcos being in danger?

"I must go," Victor said urgently. "To protect my family, to figure out what to do. But I fear ... I fear it may already be too late."

"I never wanted these things, you know," Victor continued, his voice softening. A wistful smile crossed his features. "My life here in Taos, it is *mi corazón*, my heart." He gestured expansively, as if encompassing the entire town. "The gardens I tend, the homes I fix—they are not just jobs. They are ... how do you say ... *mi pasión*."

Sam nodded unconsciously, envisioning the vibrant flowerbeds and meticulously maintained properties around town—all Victor's handiwork. His dedication was evident in every carefully pruned shrub and seamlessly repaired fence.

Victor's eyes sparked. "I will come back, I swear it. Once I unravel this mess, once I can feel safe ..." He paused, clenching his fist. "I will come back to my work, to the life I built here."

"Oh, Victor," Sam murmured, her chest tightening with empathy. She'd always known him as a hardworking, jovial presence around town. Now, seeing the depth of his commitment, the ache of his forced exile, added layers to her understanding of the man.

"I'll figure this out," she whispered fiercely to Victor's image. "Whatever's going on, whoever's behind this—I'll get to the bottom of it."

Victor's expression hardened, his dark eyes intense as he moved closer to the camera. "Whoever finds this, *por favor*, be careful. Trust no one." He glanced over his shoulder, as if expecting someone to burst in at any moment. "There are people who will do anything to become rich while they keep their secrets buried. Anything."

His voice dropped to an urgent whisper. "And if you see my Rosalita or Marcos, tell them …" Victor's voice cracked. "Tell them I love them, and I'm doing this to keep them safe."

The screen went black, leaving Sam staring at her own reflection in the dim storage unit. She blinked rapidly, stunned at the implications of Victor's warning.

"What aren't you telling me, Victor?" she murmured. "Who's really behind all this?"

She glanced at her watch, realizing how much time had passed.

"I need to talk to Beau about this," Sam decided, gathering her things and the two videotapes. Her husband's experience as sheriff might provide valuable insights. Plus, if there was a genuine threat lurking in Taos, he needed to know.

She locked up the storage unit. Had she just stepped onto a path far more dangerous than she'd anticipated? But someone had to uncover the truth.

"Oh, Victor," she said softly, looking skyward. "I won't

let you down."

Sam got into her van, a frown crossing her forehead. The late afternoon light cast long shadows across the parking lot, mirroring the doubts creeping into her mind. People could surprise you, especially when they felt cornered.

She came to a stop at the intersection of Highway 64. "Now that I know more questions to ask, I wonder if Rosalita might be able to fill in some of these blanks."

Confronting Rosalita was risky—the woman was as unpredictable as a spring storm.

"No, I'll talk to Beau first," Sam told herself firmly, accelerating when the light changed.

Sam navigated the rest of the way home to the ranch. The setting sun turned the sky peachy-gold, painting the budding fields with lines of shadow. She was so lost in thought, piecing together the puzzle of Victor's disappearance, that the sudden ping of her phone made her jump.

Pulling into their long driveway, Sam fished her phone out of her pocket. The screen glowed with a new message from an unknown number. Her brow creased as she read:

Stop digging. For your own safety, leave Victor's past buried.

A chill ran down Sam's spine, despite the mild spring air. She re-read the message. "Who could have sent this?" she muttered, glancing around. Had someone tailed her to the storage unit? The road behind her was empty, save for a stray dog trotting along the edge.

Sam's thumbs hovered over the keyboard, tempted to reply, to demand answers. But her years of working with Beau had taught her caution. Instead, she took a screenshot, her lips pressed into a thin line.

"Well," she said to herself, a wry smile tugging at the corner of her mouth, "I must be getting close to something if someone's trying to scare me off."

She pulled up to the large log house, considering her next move. The logical part of her brain whispered that maybe she should heed the warning, step back from the investigation. But the image of Victor's face on the video tape flashed in her mind—his earnest expression, the fear in his eyes.

"No," Sam decided, staring at the phone screen after turning off the engine. "Your little threat ain't gonna work, whoever you are."

The anonymous texter had made one crucial mistake— they'd only succeeded in convincing Sam that she was on the right track.

She looked around as she gathered her things, alert to any sign of someone watching. But she was alone, except for the two exuberant dogs who rushed from the porch to greet her. She ruffled their ears and laughed as they danced circles around her.

"Okay, okay. I'll get your dinner in a minute."

Her thoughts were already running ahead, trying to recall if they had a player for old videotapes. By the time she had scooped kibble for the dogs and refreshed their water bowl, she remembered coming across a VHS player on a high closet shelf. She'd intended to ask Beau if they could get rid of it, declutter a little, but something had sidetracked her at the time.

Now, she opened the closet door and spotted it. Grabbing a dining chair, she climbed up and moved some winter scarves and hats aside so she could retrieve it. Miraculously, it still had a cable attached that would connect to their TV set. It took a few minutes, but she soon had the device working and one of Victor's tapes inserted.

"Sam? What are you doing?" Beau's voice startled her, and she patted her chest to catch her breath. He was staring at the TV screen. "That's Victor. Honey, where did you get this?"

Sam paused the video and gave Beau the condensed version of how she came to learn about the storage facility and how she got inside. "We found two tapes, and they both have some startling admissions on them."

"Let's see." Bless him, he didn't make a fuss over her (probably) illegal entry into someone else's space, although Rupert had assured her that since the rent was several months overdue now, the landlord had the right to open the unit and even to sell the contents.

Together, they watched both videos all the way through.

"What do you think? He sounds really scared. And I'm confused about the part where he talks about someone taking everything, but then he wants to protect Rosalita."

Beau scratched his chin, and she gave him a couple minutes to think.

"Maybe he's trying to protect someone, someone other than Rosalita or Marcos," Sam mused quietly. "Or maybe she's more involved than he's letting on."

"Or," Beau added, "he could be a chronic worrier, or he's overdramatizing."

She nodded, remembering how Victor would often obsess over a flowerbed that wasn't getting enough water or a newly transplanted tree that wasn't flourishing as he wanted it to. The man could be described, in certain circumstances, as a worrier. But somehow she didn't think that was the case here.

Chapter 25

Sam realized neither of them had eaten in hours, so she rummaged in the freezer and came up with one of Beau's favorites that involved a large serving of mac and cheese, some hot green chile, and a couple of Italian sausage links diced up. And thank goodness for the microwave. Within fifteen minutes they were sitting down to a hearty meal, made a bit healthier with the addition of a quick green salad.

"Now that I know how your day went," he began, after taking those first few ravenous bites, "I should let you know that my day involved some good news."

She looked up, curious. "I have to know."

"The John Doe, from Cooper Ravine … we identified him. He did come from Velarde, originally, but had been living in Española. Got involved in the drug trade down there." He made a face that told her all she needed to know. The small town was a troubled place. "Once we had the Velarde lead, we checked missing person reports from around the state, got a name, and sure enough, family members had reported him gone."

"Oh, how sad." Sam set down her fork.

"Yes, it's always bittersweet news, to learn that a missing person is deceased." He met her eyes, fully aware that the same might be said about Victor Martinez—they still didn't know. "But, Sam, not knowing is always worse."

And she tended to agree with that.

"So, do you have evidence, something to make an arrest with?" she asked.

"No, and that's where this becomes good news, at least for my department. We handed over the case file and the evidence we collected to Rio Arriba County's sheriff. I know, it's tradition for each jurisdiction to want the credit for solving every case, but I don't care about grabbing any glory. I spoke with Bernie Ruiz down there—he's pretty sure he can wrap it up quickly. And that's the most important thing."

"Congratulations. I'm glad the victim's people are getting their answers."

Beau helped clear the dishes, then left to tend to something out in the barn. At least one of the horses needed new shoes, and he wanted to be sure Danny had been taking care of the stalls and monitoring their feed supply in recent weeks.

Sam re-watched the two videos but didn't gain any new insights from them. It was dark outside now, one of those clear nights with a billion visible stars, and she walked out to the back deck with her cup of tea to lean back and look skyward. Both dogs followed and settled at her side as she sank down into one of the deck chairs with a knitted afghan over her legs.

By the time her tea was gone, her early morning awakening was settling over her, a tiredness in her whole body, so she showered and headed for bed. It wasn't until she plugged her phone into its charger that she realized she'd never told Beau about the threatening text she'd received on the way home.

She studied the screen again. No more messages, and no clue where that one had come from. She had assumed the 'stop digging' threat referred to her visit to the storage unit, and the person who sent it must have seen her there.

But now that she gave it some more thought she decided it could be about her entire investigation. And that widened the field of possible senders, by quite a bit. Any of the dozens of people she'd recently spoken to about Victor might be afraid that she was getting too close to uncovering something they wanted left alone.

Sam drifted off to sleep, but her dreams were filled with faces and accusations and troubling possibilities. She startled awake, eyes wide open, her breath coming in bursts. On the other side of the bed, Beau slept peacefully. She calmed herself, trying to shove the disturbing images aside. And while the dream gradually began to fade, she realized all hope of getting back to sleep was gone.

As quietly as possible, she slid out of bed and put on her robe. Maybe some hot cocoa would do the trick. She carried her warm mug to the sofa and savored the rare treat. Unfortunately, it only served to wake her up more fully and to remind her that today was Good Friday, a busy day in Taos, especially among the Catholic population.

The Procession from San Francisco de Asis Church to the Talpa Chapel was a major event, with prayers at the 14 Stations of the Cross and family gatherings both before and after. While the grandmotherly generation traditionally did all the cooking and baking, those in the younger age groups relied on purchasing some of the foods, and the empanadas from Sweet's Sweets had become huge favorites.

Sam knew that Julio had prepared the dough for the little fruit pies in advance. But by midmorning people would begin gathering, and by midafternoon those who had walked the full journey would be hungry. She set her mug in the sink and went upstairs, where she first touched the wooden box, gathering its energy, then she pulled out her bakery attire and dressed for a long day.

She was in her van, halfway into town, when she remembered the text, which had started her disrupted night, and the fact that she hadn't shared it with Beau. Quickly, she pulled over, forwarded the screenshot to him, and asked that he call her when he received it. If things got ugly and someone confronted her, at least her law enforcement connection had some proof of the threat now.

Chapter 26

Sam had rolled out the empanada dough thin and cut perfect circles for three dozen of the little pastries when her phone rang. It was Beau and it was only 4:23 a.m. Uh-oh.

"Samantha ... what's this text message that sounds like a threat?"

"Um, yeah. I meant to tell you last night but I forgot about it until—never mind. I don't know whether to think it's something urgent or not."

"It's warning you about your own safety, Sam. Yeah, I'd take it seriously. You're at the bakery, right? Are all the doors locked?"

She walked to the back door and twisted the knob on the deadbolt. "Yes, they are." Then she put the call on speaker as she moved to the other end of the worktable to check the fruit fillings for the empanadas. The ingredients for three fruit fillings, plus dulce de leche, sat in bowls. As she spooned fruit onto one half of each pastry circle, she listened.

"This thing with Victor is escalating way beyond a few simple inquiries as to his whereabouts, Sam. I think it's time to set a trap and catch whoever's behind this."

"Honey, I have no idea who that is. Rosalita has been my main suspect all along, but now Victor's video message makes it sound like she and the nephew are also in danger."

"Which is why we can't exactly drive up to someone's house and arrest them. We need the guilty party to come to us."

Sam dropped a spoonful of pineapple filling with a clatter; a mild curse escaped her.

"Sam, what just happened?"

"Nothing. Go on."

"I'm heading for the office now, where I'm going to hold a briefing with the deputies at seven. Be there if you want to—"

"I, um … It's Good Friday."

"—or not. I can fill you in later. Mainly, I'm looking for ideas and I'll be organizing the manpower to make a capture."

She cautioned him to be careful, even as she tried to figure out how she would break away from Sweet's Sweets on one of her busiest days of the year. By the time Julio came in at six, she had a plan.

"I need to be at the sheriff's office for a couple hours this morning," she told her chief baker. "After that, I'm not sure how the day will go."

"Everything okay, boss?"

She nodded and tried to work up an encouraging smile. "It will be." She showed him the folded and crimped pastries she'd assembled already. "I need you to finish the empanadas. Remember, we usually bake some of them and fry some."

"Different customers like 'em different ways."

"Right." As he began transferring the little packets to baking sheets, she continued. "If I'm not back by the time Becky finishes her regular orders, tell her we need some fondant eggs made up for that big Easter basket cake. The customer is picking it up tomorrow, so there's still time. And anyone with extra time can make chocolate bunnies— we always seem to run out."

He nodded, sliding the first two sheets of empanadas into the pre-heated bake oven.

Sam walked into the squad room at the sheriff's office at 6:45. The coffee-scented air was filled with anticipation, although none of the deputies seemed to know specifics— just that something was up. She tapped on Beau's door to let him know she'd arrived. He seemed intent on his computer screen, but gave a nod.

She felt a bit at loose ends, not wanting to discuss anything with the deputies, unsure how much Beau might have already told them. There were the recent breakthroughs—the two videotapes, the threatening text, the conversations she'd had in the past few days. They were getting closer, that much was clear, but she didn't have any idea who was behind all this.

At three minutes before seven, Beau walked out of his office and tacked an enlarged map of Taos and the surrounding area to the bulletin board. "All right, listen up. We're initiating a sting operation today, and I need everyone on board."

He filled them in on the latest. Several of the deputies gave Sam sympathetic looks when they heard about the text message.

"We'll need time to set everything up, to lure our suspect in without their knowing anyone's watching. I don't expect a shootout, but then we never do. For that reason, I'm suggesting we get out, away from town, and we wait until late afternoon when the area should be clear."

With a pointer stick he touched an area on the map, partway out toward the airport. "There's a new development getting started out here, Blue Sage Acres. So far, just some heavy equipment and a few operators are on the site. I checked, and it looks like the workers get the afternoon off for the holiday, so it'll be a place where there won't be innocents getting in the way."

Sam edged in for a closer look.

"So, we'll have deputies stationed here, here, and here," Beau said, pointing to specific spots. "That's Rico, Harris, Maldonado, and I want you dressed like bulldozer drivers. It'll look like employees simply doing their jobs." His eyes met Sam's. "You sure you're okay with being the bait?"

Sam nodded. "I'm in, Beau. We need to catch this creep and get Victor back." Her expression betrayed none of the nerves fluttering in her stomach. It wasn't the first time she'd been present at the site of an arrest, but the stakes felt higher this time.

"All right, then," Beau continued, his voice resuming the authoritative tone he used when conveying something important. "We will maintain a perimeter around the location. State police will be watching the roads in and out, ready to blockade if I tell them it's necessary."

Sam caught his attention. "Do we know who we're looking for?"

"We've traced the number from that threatening text, but there isn't a direct connection to any of our suspects, and we can't be sure who we're dealing with."

Sam felt a mixture of frustration and admiration. Beau was nothing if not thorough in his investigations.

"The timing is crucial," Beau emphasized, straightening as he spoke. "Everyone needs to know their role inside and out. One misstep could send our suspect running."

Rico raised a hand. "Timing? When do we head out?"

"About twelve-thirty. We want the employees gone, but we need to be in place in plenty of time before we send out our invitation."

"Invitation?"

"Sam will respond to the text she received, telling the person she has evidence that can incriminate him. She says she'll show him where it is, in exchange for Victor, but they have to meet her at this location," another tap of the pointer on the map. "If they're actually holding Victor hostage—something we don't know for sure—we need to give them time to get him and drive out there, but not enough time to gather their own forces or think about retaliation. Once everything's in place, the clock starts ticking, and they'll have twenty minutes from receiving the text from Sam."

"I should actually drive out there," Sam added. "In case they're watching. I'll be in my bakery van—totally recognizable—and it's almost exactly twenty minutes from the bakery to that spot."

A frown crossed Beau's face. "I don't like that part. If someone tails you from the bakery, what's to keep him from running you off the road or waylaying you on your way to the meet-up site."

"So, then …?"

"I want you at the meeting spot when you send the text. You'll have all these sets of eyes on you. And everyone is to be armed. That goes without saying. We have no idea what lengths our suspect will go to."

Sam nodded, wondering if her unique abilities might come in handy during the operation. The thought both excited and unnerved her.

"Okay, everyone. Our designated bulldozer guys should go home at some point and get clothing that'll work for our purposes. Drive your personal vehicles. For everyone else, it's a normal day; answer calls, give out tickets … you know the drill. Past noon, I want everybody alert to the situation out at Blue Sage Acres, ready to respond in whatever way we need."

Nods all around as the deputies turned to their computers or headed out to their cruisers. Sam followed Beau into his office as the squad room cleared.

"You've got that look, Sam," Beau said softly, turning to face her. "What's going on in that brilliant mind of yours?"

She hesitated, then shook her head. "Just thinking through all the possibilities. It's a lot to take in."

Beau's warm hand found her shoulder, giving it a gentle squeeze. "We've got this, darlin'. We'll nail this guy."

Sam leaned into his touch, drawing strength from his confidence. "Beau," she began hesitantly, "I was thinking … maybe my, uh, special skills could help with the trap."

Her husband's eyebrows raised slightly, but his expression remained calm. "You mean your ability to see things others can't?"

Sam nodded, apprehension fluttering in her chest. "That other time, when we caught that art thief, I was able to see his aura before he even entered the gallery. It gave us the edge we needed."

Beau considered this, his hands resting on his desk. "It could be invaluable, Sam. But I don't want you putting yourself in harm's way."

"I know, I know," Sam replied, nodding her head. "I just hope what I'm doing will make all the difference."

* * *

It was the longest morning of her life. Sam made sugar flowers, piped cute faces on chicks and bunnies, and arranged the beautifully baked empanadas in boxes for impulse purchases. But the knowledge that she was about to take a crucial role in finding Victor and getting him home safely … that dominated her every thought as the hands on the clock crept along.

Finally, Beau texted her the come-ahead signal. She shed her baker's jacket, gathered her bag and the wooden box, along with two ancient videotapes that contained nothing. Victor's were now safely in the evidence locker at the station. She got into her bakery van and drove slowly past the sheriff's department, where Beau, in his personal pickup truck, fell in behind to tail her. They had a phone line open between them.

"You okay?" Beau asked.

Sam's eyes flicked between his truck behind her and the road ahead. "Yep. I'm good."

They drove to the north end of town, made the turn off the highway, and came to the fenced-off area that would one day be known as Blue Sage Acres. Sam could see the reason for that name—the surrounding fields were filled with sagebrush, although this particular parcel also had quite a number of piñon trees and some interesting changes in terrain. The sign at the highway promised "Luxury homes on luxurious acreage."

She wasn't sure she would go quite that far with the description. So far it was nothing but churned-up earth where the bulldozers and graders were beginning a basic layout of roads. Three pieces of heavy equipment sat at various angles, apparently parked exactly where their operators were working at the moment their holiday started. Four men in dungarees, ball caps and heavy cotton jackets mingled among the machinery. Sam had to admit that even though she knew all these deputies well, she wouldn't have recognized them right away.

She sat in her van a couple extra minutes, handling the wooden box, feeling the wood warm to her touch. She needed her senses on full alert for whatever was about to happen. She stowed the box back in her bag and stuck them safely under the seat as Beau walked up to her vehicle. He'd parked his truck behind one of the graders so it couldn't be seen from the road.

"Ready?" he asked, his hand finding hers through her open window. To fit in, he'd changed from his uniform to jeans, plaid shirt, and western boots.

Sam squeezed his hand, drawing strength from the connection. "Let's catch ourselves a culprit."

Sam stepped out of the van, breathing the crisp Taos air. She surveyed the area, her eyes narrowing as she took in every detail. Beau was already unloading equipment from the truck, his movements precise and purposeful.

"We're setting up the cameras over by those boulders," he said, nodding toward a cluster of rocks that provided natural cover. "Did you bring the bait?"

Sam nodded, holding up the fake videos and an old leatherbound notebook.

As they continued setting up, Sam's senses suddenly prickled. The air seemed to carry an energy she couldn't quite place. She paused, her hand hovering over the notebook.

Beau straightened. "All right, everyone gather 'round," he called as he walked toward the bulldozers, his voice low but authoritative.

As the team assembled, Samantha hung back, observing. Beau's presence commanded respect, his tall frame cutting a reassuring figure against the backdrop of sagebrush and the deepening blue sky.

"Listen up," Beau began, his eyes scanning the faces before him. "Our suspect is likely armed and definitely dangerous. We've got eyes on all access points, but stay alert. Remember, our priority is a clean arrest without incident."

Samantha felt a swell of pride as she watched her husband. His words instilled confidence in the team while emphasizing the gravity of the situation.

As Beau continued his briefing and the men checked to be sure their comm units were working, Samantha took a deep, cleansing breath, closing her eyes. She reached inside herself, drawing on the inner strength that had seen her through countless challenges. From reluctant caretaker to successful bakery owner, from skeptic to embracing her unique abilities—each step had led her here.

"You've got this, Sam," she whispered to herself, feeling

the familiar tingle of energy in her hands. She thought of the old woman who'd given her the antique wooden box that had changed her life, of the mysteries she'd solved, of the lifestyle she'd come to love here in Taos.

Opening her eyes, she caught Beau's gaze. He gave her a subtle nod, a silent signal to respond to the text message on her phone. Samantha stepped closer to him, squared her shoulders, and typed out the words they'd agreed upon.

The trap was set. Now they had to see who would show up.

The minutes ticked by with agonizing slowness. Samantha's eyes darted up and down the road, from the scrubby juniper bushes to the faraway buildings at the small regional airport, searching for any sign of movement. The air felt thick with tension, broken only by the occasional crackle of a radio or the soft rustle of wind through the piñon pines.

Beau crouched beside her, his body coiled with anticipation. "Anything?" he whispered, his eyes never leaving the perimeter they'd established.

Samantha shook her head, her short hair barely moving. "Not yet," she murmured. What if they didn't come? "But there's something … off. I can feel it."

She closed her eyes for a moment, reaching out with her senses. The familiar tingle crept along her skin, but the sensation was muddled, unclear.

"I wish I could pin it down," she said, frustration evident in her voice. "It's like trying to catch smoke."

Beau's hand found hers, giving it a reassuring squeeze. "You've never steered us wrong before, Sam. We'll figure it out."

Samantha met his gaze, seeing the unwavering trust

in his eyes. It struck her how far they'd come—from her initial skepticism about the powers of the wooden box to this moment of seamless partnership.

"Remember that first case we worked together?" she asked, a hint of a smile playing at her lips. "When you thought I was either crazy or hiding evidence?"

Beau chuckled softly, the sound barely audible. "Can you blame me? My by-the-book training didn't exactly cover 'psychic baker solves crimes.'"

"Hey now," Samantha retorted, her tone light despite the circumstances. "I prefer 'intuitive entrepreneur with a knack for justice.'"

Their quiet laughter faded, replaced by the watchful silence that had enveloped the area. Samantha felt a renewed sense of purpose, grateful for Beau's steadfast presence beside her.

"Whatever happens," she whispered, her eyes scanning the horizon, "we've got this."

Beau nodded, his expression serious once more. "Together," he affirmed, as they settled in to wait for the trap to spring.

"Beau," she said softly, her eyes scanning the surrounding area, catching a faint aura. "I think … I think someone's here."

Beau straightened, his hand moving toward his sidearm. "What do you mean? What are you sensing?"

Sam closed her eyes, focusing. "It's faint, but there's definitely a new presence."

She opened her eyes to find Beau watching her intently. He nodded slowly, acknowledging the importance of her insight.

"All right," he said, his voice barely above a whisper.

"We'll proceed as planned, but stay alert."

She braced herself, feeling that they were being watched. The trap was set, but she couldn't help wondering if they were the ones walking into it instead.

A sudden crackle of static from Beau's radio shattered the tense silence. Samantha's heart leapt into her throat as she saw a plume of dust. A vehicle—a pickup truck—was speeding down the road toward them. It came to an abrupt stop, a cloud of dust swirling around it.

"Be ready!" Beau's voice went out over the communication airway, authoritative and clear. "Wait until the driver moves away from his vehicle."

Sam stepped out into the open, holding the videotapes and notebook high. "Over here," she called out.

A lone figure emerged from the settling dust cloud. Where was Victor? Her message had been clear about bringing him.

Deputies materialized from their hiding spots, moving to circle the suspect. Samantha's senses went into overdrive, picking up a sickly yellow-green aura, fear and desperation radiating off the person who'd stepped out of the truck.

"Taos Sheriff's Department! Freeze!" Beau's command cut through the air.

Samantha's breath caught as she watched the scene unfold.

It was Tommy Barker.

She stepped over beside Beau in time to see Tommy handcuffed, his eyes meeting hers, filled with both anger and guilt. But there was something else in those dark eyes that didn't quite fit. Fear?

Samantha couldn't help but feel a sense of relief wash over her. Finally, they had caught the man responsible for threatening her and being involved in Victor's disappearance. But as she watched Tommy being led away by the deputies, doubts began to creep into her mind. What could have driven him to this? Was it greed? Jealousy? Or something darker lurking within his troubled heart?

"We did it," Beau said, coming to stand beside her. "You okay, Sam?"

Samantha nodded slowly. "Yeah, it's just …" She stared after the departing cruiser with Tommy Barker in the back seat. "We're missing the most important piece—Victor. We've caught the person behind the threats, but we're no closer to finding him."

Beau nodded, his expression turning serious. "You're right. This is just one piece of the puzzle."

As they walked back to her van, Samantha's mind zipped through the possibilities. "I hope Victor did as he said in the videos. Maybe he actually got away before they did something to him."

Samantha stopped, her hand on the car door. "Beau, what if there's more to this than we thought? What if the threat to me is connected to Victor's disappearance in a way we haven't considered?"

Beau considered her words. "It's possible. It is, after all, the reason we're taking Tommy in for questioning. What are you thinking?"

"I'm not sure yet," Samantha admitted, her gaze distant. "But I can't help feeling that we're still missing something vitally important."

As they drove to the sheriff's office, the quiet Taos streets passing by, Samantha knew, deep in her bones, that she wouldn't rest until Tommy revealed what had really happened to their friend.

Chapter 27

S am touched the cold glass window to the interrogation room, her eyes fixed on Tommy Barker's weary face as Beau methodically questioned him. The fluorescent lights cast harsh shadows, accentuating the lines of tension around Tommy's mouth.

They'd been at the station a couple of hours already. For lack of evidence, Beau couldn't book Tommy on suspicion of murder—at this point he was what they called a 'person of interest' and one who had a lot of explaining to do.

"So, you wanted to put Victor Martinez out of business?" Beau's voice was calm but firm. He'd changed back into his khaki uniform shirt, looking fresh and authoritative despite the long hours in his day.

Tommy shuffled in his seat, his gaze darting between

Beau and the two-way mirror. "Look, I ain't gonna lie. Victor had the market cornered on home and garden work in Taos. I wanted a piece of that pie."

Sam tried to parse the words as she listened. There was something in Tommy's tone that didn't sit right with her, a tremor of uncertainty beneath his bluster. And if that was true, why hadn't Tommy reached out to Victor's clients and attempted to book appointments the moment Victor was gone?

"You're a home builder—there's not enough money in that already? And so you wanted to expand into gardening and handyman services?" Beau pressed, leaning forward slightly.

"Yeah, that too," Tommy admitted, sitting taller in his metal chair. "But I didn't do nothing illegal, Sheriff. Just good old-fashioned competition."

"And getting rid of Victor would be the easiest path to the goal."

"I tell you, I didn't get rid of him. I don't know where he is." But his glance darted furtively to an empty corner of the room.

"It's pretty common knowledge that he's not around town anymore, and spring is normally one of his busiest seasons of the year. So, did you intend to pick up the slack, take over the landscaping market?"

Tommy shook his head.

Beau changed tactics. "You sent a threatening text to my wife, telling her to quit digging around in this case."

"No. I didn't do that."

"So, how did you know to go out there this afternoon?"

Tommy gave a long sigh. "One of my employees told me to. Said he'd received a weird text from this lady, Samantha, and I was supposed to meet her."

Beau held up a cell phone. "We traced this number, and I see it belongs to a Carlos Ruiz…"

"Right. That's who I'm talking about."

"And Carlos sent the text from this phone to my wife."

"I have no idea. What does he say about that?"

"Denies it, of course. He says he'd misplaced his phone for about half a day, so anyone could have sent the text." Beau set the phone on the table. "That much could be true. Which leads us right back to you. You're the logical one who would have found Carlos's phone lying around someplace, you used it to send the text and figured no one would put it together."

As Beau continued his questioning, Sam felt her skepticism meter rise. Tommy's professional jealousy explained some things, but something told her there was more to the story than a misplaced phone and a conniving plan to scare her with a text message. And who did she know who was a supreme conniver?

She stepped away from the glass and turned to Rico, who was monitoring the interrogation with her. She told him to let Beau know what she was doing next.

"Will do, Sam. Our suspect will be here until we get some answers. That holding cell has a nice, comfy cot in it."

The sun had set, leaving an orange glow on the western horizon and Sam found herself standing before Rosalita's modest adobe home, her heart pounding with apprehension. They still didn't know for a fact whether Victor was alive or not.

Sam raised her hand to knock on the bright blue door. As her knuckles met the weathered wood, she hoped she still had some residual energy with which to detect the woman's aura.

"You can do this, Sam," she murmured to herself, squaring her shoulders.

The door creaked open, revealing Rosalita, who was wearing a loose caftan. Her expression flickered from surprised to guarded as she gripped the door. "Sam. What brings you here?"

"Good evening, Rosalita," Sam replied, trying to keep her voice steady. "I was hoping we could talk a bit more about what's going on with Victor. May I come in?"

Rosalita's eyes squinted. "You have a letter from my lawyer."

"I know. But, in the long run don't we both just want what's best for Victor?" Even as she said it, Sam realized that might not be Rosalita's intent at all.

But the woman relented and stepped back to admit her to the house. As Sam crossed the threshold, she caught the faint aroma of something spicy simmering in the kitchen.

"Sit, sit," Rosalita said, gesturing toward the worn sofa with deliberate, slightly defensive movements. Her eyes darted around the room as if checking for anything out of place.

Sam lowered herself onto the sofa, noting how Rosalita chose to remain standing. The casual stance was at odds with the nervous energy radiating from her.

"Something smells delicious," Sam commented, trying to ease the tension. "Are you cooking?"

Rosalita's eyes narrowed slightly. "Just a little something. Now, what more did you want to know about Victor? I've already told you everything."

Sam held her gaze steady. There was a faint aura surrounding the woman. "I think we both know that's not entirely true, Rosalita. Beau is questioning a suspect right now. I'm here to help, but I need the whole story."

Rosalita relaxed enough to take a seat in a chair across from Sam.

"It must be difficult for you," Sam probed gently. "Being separated for so long. Have you spoken with him recently?"

Rosalita's eyes darted away, her aura flaring with a slight burst of yellow. "*Sí*, of course. Just last week. He's … improving."

Sam nodded, noticing her hesitation, feeling like she was on the right track. The idea of Victor abandoning his life and work in Taos without a word to anyone seemed increasingly implausible.

"We all want to help, if we can. Is there anything you haven't mentioned that might give us a clue about what's really going on?"

Rosalita's hands twitched in her lap, her eyes darting to the kitchen and back. "I … I don't know what you mean," she said, but her voice wavered. "I've told you everything."

Everything? Hardly. Sam wanted to confront her about the phone call she'd overheard, about the sale of the house, not to mention things other people had told her. But at this moment, her main concern was to locate Victor and bring him home.

Sam could see the cracks forming in Rosalita's façade. She pressed gently, "Are you sure? Could someone have taken him away? Even the smallest detail could be important. We just want to make sure Victor is safe."

Rosalita's composure slipped further, her aura pulsing with conflicting emotions. "He is safe," she insisted, but the tremor in her voice betrayed her uncertainty. "He must be."

Must be? Sam wanted to leap on that statement, but if

she pushed too hard, Rosalita might shut down completely. Then again, if she didn't push enough, this opportunity could slip away. *Take the sympathetic stance, resist the urge to throttle her.*

"Rosalita," Sam said gently, "I can see this is troubling you. We all care about Victor, and about you too."

Rosalita's eyes glistened with unshed tears, her carefully constructed narrative beginning to crumble. Her shoulders slumped, the fight draining out of her as she met Sam's gaze. For a moment, the cunning mask slipped, revealing a flicker of vulnerability beneath.

"I …" Rosalita began, her voice barely above a whisper. She swallowed hard. "I made mistakes, Señora Sam. Terrible mistakes."

Sam kept her voice soft, encouraging. "It's okay, Rosalita. We all make mistakes. Can you tell me about them?"

Rosalita's hands twisted in her lap, her dark hair falling forward to partially obscure her face. "Victor and I, we fought so much. I wanted more—more money, a bigger house. But he was content with his simple life. He said he was taking care of our future." Her voice trembled. "I pushed him, threatened him. I thought … I thought I could make him see things my way."

Sam scrambled to process this unexpected candor. She fought to keep her expression neutral, not wanting to interrupt Rosalita's flow of confession.

"I never meant for it to go this far," Rosalita continued, a tear finally escaping down her cheek. "I love Victor, I really do. But my anger, my desires … it ruined everything between us."

"What happened, Rosalita?" Sam prompted gently.

"Where is Victor now?"

Rosalita looked up, her eyes full of regret. "I don't know, Señora. That's the truth. He left after our last fight, and I haven't seen him since. I've been lying, pretending, because I was afraid … afraid of what people would think, afraid of what might have happened to him because of me."

"What about the text messages you showed me, the phone calls you've told me about?"

"Those are real. But you asked *where* he is, and he has not shared that." Her fingers twisted in a painful-looking grip. "The phone number I have is in Mexico. That's all I know. He calls me. That is the arrangement."

Sam felt a pang of empathy, even as her investigator side catalogued this new information. She reached out, hesitantly patting Rosalita's hand. "Thank you for telling me the truth. It's an important first step. Now, let's see if we can figure out what really happened to Victor, okay?"

The woman nodded, a tear dripping from her chin.

"Rosalita, I understand this is difficult, but I need to know more about Victor's last days here. Who did he see? Where did he go?"

Rosalita seemed to deflate as she sighed. "He was working at the Freeman place, fixing their roof before winter. And … and he mentioned meeting with that carpenter, Tommy Barker."

Sam's eyebrows rose slightly. "Did Victor say what that was about?"

"No, no details. Just that Tommy had approached him about working together on something big. Victor didn't like the idea. He prefers to work alone."

Sam worked to connect this new information with

what she knew about Tommy's ambitions. She kept her voice gentle, "Did Victor seem especially worried about that meeting, or anything else, in those last days?"

Rosalita shook her head. "No, he was … happy, looking forward to the holidays. But he was not talking much about his work anymore. It was strange."

"Rosalita, I need to ask—did Tommy Barker ever threaten you? Or Victor?"

Rosalita's eyes widened in genuine surprise. "Threaten? No, *nunca*. Why would you think that?"

Sam watched Rosalita's face carefully. But she saw only confusion in the older woman's demeanor.

"It's just part of the investigation," Sam said smoothly, her brain already churning over what this might mean. If Tommy hadn't threatened Rosalita or Victor, what was his true role in all of this?

"Rosalita," Sam said, her voice warm, "thank you for being so open with me. Your honesty means more than you know." She reached out, hesitating for a moment before gently patting Rosalita's hand. "Everything you've shared is crucial in our search for Victor."

Rosalita offered a small, wavering smile. "I hope … I hope it helps, Señora Sweet. Victor, he is a good man. Despite our *peleas* … our fights."

Sam nodded, rising from her seat. "We're doing everything we can to find him and sort this out. Your cooperation is invaluable."

Sam offered a reassuring smile as she walked toward the door. "We'll be in touch if we need anything. And Rosalita? If you remember anything else, anything at all, please don't hesitate to call me or Sheriff Cardwell."

Stepping outside, Sam paused. *What am I missing?* she

wondered as she walked to her van. *There's still a piece of this puzzle that doesn't fit.*

"Okay, Sam," she muttered to herself, "let's break this down." She pulled away from the house and steered toward Paseo del Pueblo Sur. "Victor's last known activities, the people he interacted with before disappearing. And Rosalita's reaction to Tommy Barker ..."

Interesting, this new, forthcoming side of Rosalita. She'd detected slight flickers of dishonesty at the beginning of their conversation. But there was something else, too. A genuine caring for Victor that couldn't be faked.

And what Tommy had said during the interview with Beau, about wanting a piece of the local landscaping and home repair business ... but then it sounded like Victor's response to that proposal was resistance. Surely that wasn't enough to make him leave town. But was it enough to make Barker want to do away with him?

"What am I missing?" Sam asked the empty van, frustration creeping into her voice. "There's got to be a connection I'm not seeing."

At least she felt a little closer to the answers than she'd been yesterday.

Chapter 28

She was approaching the plaza when she felt the tug of the bakery. A glance at her dashboard clock told her it was already past closing time. The employees had probably left for the day, but Sam realized she'd hardly been there all day. It would be a good idea to stop in, just make sure she wouldn't be needed early in the morning. The concept of sleeping in tomorrow sounded wonderful to her at this moment.

She made the left turn just before the plaza entrance and wound her way to the parallel street where she spent so much of her life nowadays. Soft night lights were on inside the bakery. Next door, Puppy Chic was dark. Ivan's car sat in front of Mysterious Happenings and she saw him lock the front door of the bookshop, preparing to leave.

Sam pulled around to the back alley, hoping to avoid

conversation. All she wanted right now was to check the day's receipts and take a look over tomorrow's orders. The Saturday before Easter Sunday would be a busy one. Then she would beat a swift retreat to home and bed. She sent Beau a text: Quick stop at the bakery before heading home. Interesting talk with Rosalita to tell you about. I promise, no baking but if I'm not home in 20 min, send the troops! LOL

She got out of the van. As she fumbled for her shop keys in the dim light, a muffled thud echoed from behind the adjacent bookshop.

Sam froze, her senses on high alert. A cat, apparently rummaging in the boxes Ivan had set out for the trash collector, ran toward the fence that separated the alley from the other businesses behind. She relaxed.

Until a figure emerged from the shadows. Sam felt the hairs on her neck stand up.

The glow of a nearby streetlamp revealed Talia Simpson's wild blonde curls. The Realtor's eyes darted back and forth, her usual confident demeanor replaced by visible anxiety.

Sam's heart thudded.

"Talia, what are you doing out here?" Sam called out, keeping her voice steady. In an alley behind a string of businesses. "Is everything okay?"

Talia startled, her turquoise jewelry jangling as she spun to face Sam. "Oh! Samantha, I didn't see you there." Her laugh sounded forced, almost manic. "Just … checking on a property. You know how it is when you own a business— always on the clock!"

Sam's phone pinged with an incoming text. Beau's number appeared. LOL? You never say that. Everything okay?

Sam took a step back, eyeing the real estate agent who was staring at her, noting how Talia's hands shook as she clutched her designer handbag. "At this hour? That's dedication."

"Well, when duty calls …" Talia's smile didn't reach her eyes. She glanced toward the door to the bakery's storeroom.

Could Talia possibly know what Sam had found in there?

Sam's phone pinged again: **Sam? Worrying here!**

"Talia, 'scuse me a second …" She typed a quick reply: **SOS at bakery!!!!!**

"Sorry. Husband wondering if he's supposed to pick up the pizza."

Then she touched Beau's number in her contacts, opening a line and keeping it open, her screen facing away from the woman who was less than twenty feet away.

"Actually, Talia, I'm glad I ran into you," Sam said, leaning against the bumper of her van with feigned casualness, taking a big guess as she posed a question. "I've been meaning to ask—how are things going with that project? The one you said Victor was working on?"

Talia's face hardened, her earlier nervousness giving way to a flash of anger. "That old fool? I wouldn't bring him in on anything big. Please. I told you, I'm done dealing with his shoddy workmanship and missed deadlines on the little things."

Sam raised an eyebrow, carefully cataloging Talia's reaction as she came up with another contentious question. "Oh? I'd heard it was a pretty big deal. Did something change?"

Talia's lips pressed into a thin line. "Let's just say we had … differences. But that's all in the past now."

The hairs on the back of Sam's neck stood up. There was something ominous in Talia's tone, a hint of finality that sent a chill down her spine.

"In the past?" Sam pressed, fighting to keep her voice neutral as she kept the woman talking. "What exactly do you mean by that, Talia?"

The wail of a siren drifted on the night air. Talia's face drained of color, her earlier audacity evaporating in an instant.

"I ... I have to go," she stammered, already backing away. "Early showing tomorrow. You understand."

"No, really, I'm curious about what you meant." Sam stepped forward, carefully probing. "Sounds like you knew Victor wouldn't be around."

The siren passed by, into the distance.

"Just ... creative differences," Talia said, relaxing slightly. "You know how particular certain clients can be about renovations. Sometimes it's hard to meet everyone's expectations."

Sam's paranormal sight was fading but she caught the faint trace of an aura now, a sickly yellow glow tinged with flashes of deep crimson. Sam's breath caught in her throat; she'd never seen an aura change so rapidly or flash with different colors like this. It spoke volumes about Talia's emotional state—fear, guilt, and a desperate need for self-preservation all swirling together.

Before Sam could process this new information, the alley was suddenly bathed in pulsing blue lights. Sheriff's Department cruisers arrived at both ends, their silent approach unnoticed in the heat of the confrontation. Relief washed over Sam, knowing Beau had heard everything through the open phone line.

Talia's eyes darted wildly, the realization of her predicament setting in. "Wait!" she cried out, her voice shrill with panic. "You don't understand. It was all Tommy's idea! He's the one who threatened Victor, not me. I was just supposed to look through Victor's toolbox for some kind of videotape!"

Well, that explained what she was doing lurking behind the bakery just now. Sam stood her ground, unfazed by Talia's desperate attempt to deflect blame. "Nice try, Talia, but I heard you admit your involvement. You and Tommy were in this together."

"No, you're twisting my words!" Talia insisted. "I never wanted anyone to get hurt. Tommy, he … he has a temper. Things got out of hand!"

Sam's eyes narrowed, her voice steady. "Out of hand how, Talia? What exactly happened to Victor?"

Beau got out of his cruiser, but Sam held up a hand to make him pause.

Talia's lower lip quivered, but before she could respond, Sam pressed on. "We have evidence linking you both to Victor's disappearance. He recorded messages, and it all points to you and Tommy trying to force Victor out of business."

"You don't know anything!" Talia spat, but her nerve was crumbling fast.

Okay, technically true. Sam could only hope her guesses were accurate.

For a moment, the only sound in the alley was the low hum of the cruisers' engines. Sam held her breath, silently praying that Talia would make the right choice.

The scrape of boots on asphalt broke the tense silence as Sheriff Beau Cardwell approached, his tall figure casting a long shadow in the dim alley light. His authority brought an immediate change in the atmosphere.

"Talia," Beau's voice was firm but calm, his stare locked on the trembling real estate agent. "Show your hands. Let's talk this through."

Sam felt a surge of relief at her husband's arrival, but kept her focus on Talia. Fear and desperation seemed to radiate off her in waves.

Talia's voice wavered. "I … I didn't mean for it to go this far," she whispered, her wild blonde curls falling across her face. "Tommy said we'd just scare Victor a little, make him see reason."

"And what reason was that?" Beau asked, taking another measured step forward.

"The high-end market," Talia's voice cracked. "We wanted to corner it. Victor … he wouldn't play ball. Wouldn't partner up."

Partners? Pieces started clicking into place. "So you decided to take him out of the equation entirely?"

Talia's shoulders slumped, the fight draining out of her. "I never wanted him dead."

Chapter 29

Sam's heart sank.

As Deputy Rico moved in to handcuff Talia, Sam exchanged a glance with Beau. The relief of Talia's admission was tempered by their fear for Victor's fate.

"Where is he, Talia?" Sam pressed, her heart pounding. "Where's Victor?"

"Tommy … he went too far. I was just trying to save my business, I swear." Talia's tear-streaked face crumpled. "The old Sanchez place," she whispered. "Toward the ski valley road. I think that's where he took him. He said there's a root cellar."

Sam's breath caught. Could Victor have survived that kind of months-long ordeal?

She watched as Rico escorted their suspect to his vehicle, and the squad car's taillights disappeared around the corner. The cool night air sent a chill over her skin.

"We need to move fast, Beau," she said, turning to her husband. Her voice was steady, but her eyes betrayed the depth of her fears. "If Victor's been in that root cellar all this time …"

Beau nodded, his expression grim. "I'll radio for several cars and an ambulance. I'll send them out there now. You and I should go to the station while we've got both Tommy and Talia in custody."

Leaving her van at the bakery, she climbed into the passenger seat of Beau's cruiser. Her gaze swept over the darkened adobe buildings lining the street. The town she loved suddenly felt different, harboring secrets she was only beginning to unravel.

"You okay, Sam?" Beau asked, starting the engine.

She turned to him, her face solemn. "I will be when we find Victor. Preferably alive and in one piece."

As they drove toward the station, Sam wondered what other secrets were waiting to be uncovered. Beau led the way in through the back entrance, traversing the squad room and calling out to Rico.

"Who's headed out to the Sanchez place?"

"Walters, Harris, and Ortiz, boss."

"Good. Did you put Talia Simpson in one of the interrogation rooms?"

At Rico's nod, Beau signaled for the deputy to follow. "Good. I want Tommy Barker out of the holding cell. Put him in the other interrogation room."

Rico jumped up and left the room.

"Sam, you want to be in with one of the suspects, or just listen in?

"How about if I listen to both sets of questions and

answers at the beginning. Then, if I see something where I might contribute, I'll step in there with you."

"Good plan." He took her elbow and they walked to the monitoring space between the two bare-bones interrogation spaces.

Talia was pacing the floor in Room A, edgy as a cat. Beau switched on the recording equipment and turned the microphone volumes up so Sam could hear everything. In under two minutes, Rico opened the door to Room B and ushered Tommy inside. Their suspect seemed sullen, maybe a little groggy, as if he'd been wakened from a nap.

"I'll start with Tommy," Beau told her. "See if what Talia told us gets a rise out of him. We can let her stew for a while. She's gotta be pretty freaked out about what we'll find in that root cellar."

So am I, Sam admitted to herself.

She watched her husband walk into Room B and take a stance, towering over Tommy who was slumped in a chair. After a minute of this silent intimidation, he circled the table and sat down, laying his hands on a file folder that, in reality, only contained his quickly jotted notes about what Talia had admitted to Sam earlier.

"So, Tommy. The Sanchez place, and the root cellar out there. Want to share anything with me about that?"

Tommy blanched, his dark hair stark against the pallor of his skin.

"My men are on the way out there now. Are they going to find the body of Victor Martinez?"

"What? No!"

"Talia Simpson told us you took Victor out there. Was the idea just to intimidate him into going along with the property scheme? Or was it better to simply kill him and be rid of the obstacle to your plans, once and for all?"

Tommy was sitting bolt upright in the chair now. His eyes darted back and forth. Sam could practically read his mind. How much had Talia told them, he was surely wondering.

It didn't take long for Tommy to cave. "It was all Talia's idea. God, I can't believe I ever found that woman attractive."

Beau's head cocked to one side. "Go ahead."

"We met about two years ago, right after she came to town. She, with her real estate license and big plans … I guess she thought teaming up with the primo young contractor in town would be her ticket to riches. I don't know. I was just flattered that she'd chosen me to sleep with her and to be the sole contractor for this big development. She said she already had all the details nailed down for Blue Sage Acres, and if I could get house plans drawn up for two or three custom, high-end houses we'd be on our way."

Beau was making notes as Tommy talked. "Are you a home designer, too?"

Tommy shook his head. "I hired a firm out of Santa Fe. Big money out of pocket. Those designs ate up everything I'd made on my last two custom builds."

"But you were going to get it all back, and then some."

"Right. Except I never saw a penny, at least not yet." He fidgeted in his seat. "Other than us inviting Victor in on the deal, to provide landscape plans and create fabulous gardens for the new places, I don't see what he has to do with this."

"It must have been important enough that you felt you had to take him away and stash him in a root cellar." Beau leaned forward, putting on the intimidation once again.

"No, I swear. That was just Talia's idea of a little scare tactic. Leave him there a few days and he'd come around to an agreement."

"But …?"

"Next time I went out to take him some food, he was gone. I just figured he'd show up in town and report what we'd done."

"Why scare him? If he said no to providing the landscapes for the new homes, why not just find someone else?"

Tommy shrugged. "You'd have to ask Talia about that. By that time, last fall, I was feeling like I'd been caught up in a tornado. I needed the work, I'd already sunk my own money into it, and at that point I was just tossed into whatever it was Talia wanted to do next."

Beau sat back, his mouth a straight line, letting the flimsiness of that excuse echo through the room. He stood and walked to the door, giving Tommy a sharp stare before he walked out. The click of the lock came through loud and clear.

Sam turned toward the door to the monitoring room as Beau peeked his head in. "Does that fit with what you know so far?"

"I guess, Beau. I didn't get anything from Victor's notes about Blue Sage Acres, but it does make sense."

"Okay. I'm going to step across and get the other version."

Sam turned to watch as Beau stepped into Room A. Talia's pacing came to an abrupt halt.

"It's about time, Sheriff. Why am I being held here?"

Sam felt her mouth fall open. *Aside from admitting to me that you and Tommy had done away with Victor?*

Beau indicated one of the chairs, inviting her to sit. "Until we verify that Tommy Barker was solely responsible for taking Victor Martinez to a remote root cellar and leaving him there, we still have questions for you."

Talia took the usual plea. "Of course, Sheriff, I want to do anything I can to help."

"Blue Sage Acres. Tell me about that."

Her version agreed with Tommy's, leaving out the parts about his having to foot the bill for the house plans and his feeling she had used him.

"And Victor Martinez. He didn't want to be a part of it, so how is that a reason you needed him gone?"

Talia's eyes narrowed. She knew they'd talked to Tommy, but she had no idea how much he'd admitted. She took the defensive. "It wasn't my idea to get rid of Victor. That's all on Tommy. We had words, and the last I knew about it, Tommy was going to keep checking on Victor, taking him food and water, until he came around to our way of thinking."

"Thinking that he should be forced into doing the landscaping for your project? Sorry Ms. Simpson, how does that actually make any sense?"

She drummed her nails on the tabletop, her mouth pursed.

Beau looked up, toward the mirrored glass on the wall, and gave Sam a short nod. She clipped her deputy's badge to her waistband, gathered her bag and walked into the room. Talia seemed surprised to see her there. Sam looked toward Beau. "Are we discussing the evidence now?"

He nodded.

"I understand some of what you're going through," Sam said turning toward the suspect sympathetically, buying time as she formulated her next move. "The high-end market must be especially challenging. All those luxury properties and demanding clients …"

Sam reached into her bag, pulling out Victor's notebook.

"Talia, I found something interesting in Victor's storage unit," she said, her voice calm but firm. "There were some tapes and documents …"

Talia's face paled, her wild blonde curls seeming to droop. "Oh? I'm sure that's all standard paperwork."

"Not quite," Sam countered, opening the notebook. "Some of Victor's more cryptic notes are beginning to make sense, now that we know more about your development plans. Looks like someone was skimming off the top, inflating costs. Victor figured it out and, well, let's say he was feeling intimidated. Scared enough to write down a lot of things."

Talia's fear began radiating off her in waves. "That's … that's ridiculous," she stammered, eyes darting around the room. "Victor must have made a mistake."

"I don't think so," Sam pressed, throwing in some information based on pure deduction. "His records were meticulous. And there's more—communications between you and Tommy Barker, discussing ways to … how did you put it? 'Take what we need from the old man'?"

"You don't understand," Talia hissed. "Victor was holding us back. Tommy and I had plans, *big* plans, for Taos real estate. But that stubborn old fool wouldn't play ball. His house alone is now worth a fortune, and Rosalita had the paperwork to help—." She stopped talking abruptly.

"Talia, it's going to go a lot easier on you if you share information with us. What did you do?"

"We … we just wanted to scare him, make him see

reason. But things got out of hand. Tommy, he … he has a temper."

The implications of Talia's words hit Sam like a punch to the gut. Poor Victor. She prayed he was still alive, but the sinking feeling in her stomach told her Tommy could have absolutely lied about everything.

Talia's voice wavered, a desperate edge creeping in. "You don't understand, Samantha. This town is changing. The high-end market is booming, and we needed to adapt. Victor was … he was a relic."

Sam kept her voice steady. "So, you and Tommy decided to take matters into your own hands? Corner the market by force?"

"It wasn't like that," Talia protested, but her conviction was crumbling. "We were going to offer him a partnership. Rentals, handyman services, landscaping—a complete package for wealthy out-of-towners. But Victor, he was so stubborn!"

Sam's eyes narrowed. "And when he refused?"

"We … we thought we could pressure him. Show him the writing on the wall."

"Victor built his business on trust and quality work," Sam countered. "He wouldn't throw that away for a get-rich-quick scheme."

Talia's face contorted. "You don't know what it's like, struggling in this town! Victor had it easy, everyone loved him. Tommy and I, we saw an opportunity …"

Sam felt a surge of anger. "An opportunity to destroy a man's life? Victor was part of this community. His family has been here at least three generations. His home is not a property to get rich from. The thing a lot of newcomers don't understand is that New Mexico is not a big-developer friendly place, for this very reason. We cherish our heritage. We don't want our small towns turned into 'visions' that appeal to big-city folks. Victor has always been very much a part of that."

She stopped short, a chilling realization dawning. "Talia, what's the connection? Starting a new development and trying to get his cooperation is one thing, but there's more, isn't there?"

The realtor's eyes went wide, fear replacing defiance. In that moment, Sam knew they had crossed a line from which there was no return. But she was still missing something crucial.

A knock sounded on the door.

Chapter 30

When Beau opened the door, Rico summoned him out to the hallway. Sam closed the notebook and followed. They stepped away a short distance from both interrogation rooms.

"Boss, Walters and Harris found the root cellar at the Sanchez place."

"And?"

"No sign of Victor Martinez. In fact, no sign that anyone spent any time there. At least not recently. They're searching the rest of the property now, but so far not turning up any evidence."

Sam looked up at Beau. "So, we're back to square one— No, wait. We know there's more. And I think I know who can fill in the blanks, but I need your help, Beau. She's figured out how to dodge around me."

He knew exactly who she was talking about. "Rico, put Tommy Barker back in the holding cell. Offer Ms. Simpson coffee or water or something, but keep her right where she is." He turned back to Sam. "Let's go put the fear in Rosalita Suarez. We'll get the answers to this whole mess, right now."

Lights were on inside Rosalita's house, a good sign. Beau pulled into the driveway behind her car, blocking it in. When Sam knocked on the door, it opened almost immediately. Victor's ex-wife must have seen their lights when they arrived.

"Señora Sam, what a surprise to see you!" The fake smile revealed that odd gold tooth. Rosalita's gaze dropped to Sam's belt and she took a step back when she saw the badge.

Beau didn't give her a chance to close the door. "Ms. Suarez, we have questions. You can answer them here or you can come with us down to my office."

Rosalita stepped aside and invited them in. Beau matter-of-factly circled the living room, peering into the other rooms that branched out from it. Assured that no one else was there, he walked up to Rosalita, backing her toward the sofa.

"Talia Simpson and Tommy Barker are in interrogation rooms at my office right now," he began. "An interesting story has emerged, about them pressuring Victor, wanting to involve him in a business deal that he wanted no part of."

Rosalita looked away.

"We've sent a team out to search the place where we heard they took Victor's body. The Sanchez place out near the ski valley road."

"Oh, my poor Victor. I can't believe it." By now

Rosalita was wringing her hands, working up some tears.

"Cut it out, Rosalita. You knew about this all along," Sam interjected. "I found tapes Victor made and notebooks detailing his thoughts, all made before he disappeared. Your getting his power of attorney has a lot to do with this, doesn't it?"

A flicker of fear crossed the woman's face.

Before she could invent another excuse, Beau jumped in. "Where is Victor's body, Rosalita? Keep in mind that your answer could put you in prison if we find him somewhere else."

At the mention of doing hard time, her reserves crumpled completely. She broke down in sobs, waving a hand in front of her teary eyes. "I have told you the truth, Miss Sam, Victor is in Mexico. He is!"

"Because he's so ill he can't find decent medical treatment closer to home?" Sam's sarcasm cut the air.

"Because he is hiding from them. It was not safe for him to be here."

Beau sat up straighter in the chair facing their witness. "I want proof of life, Rosalita, and I want it now. No more text messages that happened weeks ago, no more 'sorry, the line is busy.' If you are in touch with Victor, as you've told Sam, then you need to get him on the phone now. This minute."

"Si, okay." She began to rise from her seat. "The phone is on my dresser."

Beau tilted his head toward Sam. "Go with her."

With the phone in hand, Sam followed Rosalita back to the living room. "It's a Mexican cell phone, with the Telcel service there. We use prepaid cards."

Which explained why neither Sam nor any of Victor's

other local customers had been able to reach him at his normal number.

"Dial it." Beau's face was hard, his voice firm.

With shaking hands, Rosalita started to go to the menus. "He will not answer. That is the arrangement. He only calls me."

"Fine. Send him a text and tell him to call. It's urgent."

"Make it a video call," Sam suggested. "I want to hear his voice and see his face."

"Ah. Facetime. Yes."

Sam watched over her shoulder while Rosalita sent the text. Within two minutes, her Facetime app lit up.

"Rosy? *Que es?*

When Sam saw Victor's face on the screen, she nearly cried with relief.

"Ella quiere hablar contigo," said Rosalita, handing the phone over to Sam.

Victor's face lit up. "You wanted to talk with me, Señora Sam? *Como estas?*"

"I'm fine now, Victor. And you? Have you been ill?"

He assured her he was perfectly healthy, although eager to come home.

"A lot of people in Taos will be happy to know you are safe. And we all want you back home. Our gardens have missed you." They shared a little chuckle over that.

"Ay, what was I thinking?" he muttered to himself, shaking his head. "Leaving like a thief in the night. Sam, *mi amiga*, you must be so worried."

Beau stepped in beside Sam, eager to speak with the subject of the huge search. "Victor, we're trying to put together the story of what Tommy Barker and Talia Simpson are up to, and it somehow involved you. We were afraid they had killed you."

"Ay, it could have happened that way. Tommy, he took me out to the old Sanchez place—maybe you know it? He left me in a cellar with my hands tied, and then he said he would come the next day with food and water. But I heard them talking, him and the lady with the curly yellow hair. They wanted my land."

"Wait—what land?" Sam asked.

"Out west of the town. Near the road to the airport. My family owns one hundred acres out there, since my grandfather."

Blue Sage Acres. Sam and Beau exchanged a look. This was the bigger picture, far bigger than a landscaping contract.

Rosalita was edging toward the door, Sam realized, and she gave Beau a nudge to stop her. "*Uno momento*, Victor," she said.

"Rosalita, we'll need to talk more about this at my office," Beau said, grabbing handcuffs from his belt. "Sam, learn what you can. We'll be waiting in the car."

Once she was alone in Rosalita's living room, Sam asked the two most important questions. "Victor, did you sign a paper called a power of attorney for Rosalita?"

"Oh, *si*. So she could pay my bills and set up appointments for my customers."

And so much more. Sam tried to refrain from rolling her eyes.

"Okay, we'll ask her more about that, Victor. I have to know—after Tommy took you to the cellar at the Sanchez place … how long were you there? Did he let you out later?"

"Oh, no, Señora Sam. Victor may be a simple person,

pero I am *no estupido*." He smiled, his genuine, beautiful smile. "I know, when someone ties your hands and leaves you in the dark, it is not the time to wait around for them. I untied the ropes with my teeth." He gave a toothy grin.

Sam smiled, despite the frightening situation. "So, you got away before he ever came back?"

"*Sí.* I got to a house with lights on, asked them for a ride home. From there, I take some things, some clothes, walk through town to the bus station. It was not far. A bus to El Paso, then across the border, and then to my cousin's house."

So Rosalita had been telling the truth, somewhat, all along.

"I should have said something, anything," he told her, his brow furrowing. "Left a note, made a call. *Dios mío*, what must everyone think of me now?"

Victor's eyes misted over as he told of the menacing words, the implied violence. He swallowed hard, pushing the memories aside. "I didn't want to put Rosalita or Marcos in danger, but I should have told someone, like you and Sheriff Beau. You have always been good to me, like family. I just … I panicked."

"It's all right, Victor. We can handle it from here. And I think it's safe for you to come home now, whenever you're ready."

Chapter 31

Easter Sunday dawned clear and crisp, with dew on the grass and the promise of flowering gardens soon to burst into bloom. Sam and Beau had been invited to go with Kelly's family to an Easter sunrise church service followed by an egg hunt, but Sam begged off. Friday night had turned into Saturday morning at Beau's office, as their set of suspects were questioned and the story gradually came out. Saturday was another long day that disappeared in a blur, between the bakery and the sheriff's department, and Sam was exhausted.

She felt as if she'd barely had time for a shower before they were due at Kelly's house for the midday Easter dinner. They drove up to the classic Victorian home, pulling under the portico near the side entrance. Sam held an oversized Easter egg cake, specifically what Ana had asked for, weeks ago. She sent a special thank-you toward Becky for doing the bulk of the work on it. Considering how crazy the past two days had become, the cake would not have been finished otherwise.

Ana met them at the door, shrieking when she saw the cake. "It's the best one *ever*, Grammie. I love it!" As she chattered on about this morning's egg hunt (also the best one *ever!*), Kelly led the way and placed the gorgeous pastry as the centerpiece on the table.

Zoë stood at the kitchen stove, stirring something that smelled wonderful, but she set her spoon aside and rushed over to hug both Sam and Beau. "I heard that Victor's on his way home. You have to give us the details."

"He is. He's on the bus now, even though I offered to get him a plane ticket. Says he likes having the time to think."

"I just hope Rosalita is paying the price for all she put him through," Zoë said, now gripping her wooden spoon like a weapon.

"It's a little more complicated than we thought." Sam pitched in and helped arrange ham slices on a platter. Beau quickly figured out that Scott and Darryl had found a baseball game, a spring training special, so he made his way to the parlor where the television captured all three of the men.

"But Rosalita was involved, wasn't she?" Kelly asked. "We had that … message … that a family deception was at the heart of it."

"*Lots* of it. That's true. Rosalita has softened up quite a bit, and I think she genuinely cares for Victor, in her own self-centered, prickly way. I don't know if they'll end up back together, but it doesn't sound like Victor's holding a grudge."

Zoë sighed. "He's just the sweetest man."

"He really is. Even with Talia Simpson and Tommy Barker, two people against whom he legitimately could press charges, I don't think he's going to. Beau has been firm that he'll be keeping a super sharp eye on them both."

Kelly reached into the fridge and brought out a fancy plate filled with deviled eggs, handing it off to Sam to carry to the table. "What about Victor's nephew, Marcos? I heard he left town."

"He's back. He came walking into the station about the same time Beau was taking Rosalita's statement. You know what he said? 'Oh sorry, I didn't realize I was bothering anyone. I just needed some me-time.' What the—"

"Right? So, it sounds like he's as selfish as ever."

"Definitely. We talked to Victor a second time, as he was leaving Mexico. He realizes his nephew will probably never be willing to do the hard work of gardening, so his idea of training him and then leaving him the business someday … doesn't look like that will happen. But he sounds fine with letting go of that plan and moving on."

Zoë scooped her sautéed veggie medley into a serving bowl, and Sam took the maple-baked sweet potatoes out of the oven. With the ham, two more side dishes, and a basket of rolls, the big meal was complete.

"Ana, go tell your daddy and the other guys that dinner is served," Kelly called out. In the background they could hear the little girl repeat the invitation verbatim.

A hush fell over the group as they filled their plates and took those first mouthwatering bites. But once the initial hunger was sated, everyone had questions about the complicated mess that had befallen their favorite gardener and handyman.

Sam deferred to Beau, since she hadn't actually sat in on all of the interrogations.

"Basically, Talia Simpson decided to remake this little town into her idea of what a resort should be."

Zoë sputtered. "She hadn't yet figured out that we're extremely resistant to that kind of development around here?"

"She knows it now." Beau smiled as he described the fit she threw as she announced she was leaving this 'loser little town' (he even drew out the air quotes). "She's closing her office this week and heading back to Florida, where she can make more money and fits in better with the people."

"That note I found in Victor's toolbox," Sam added. "I thought when he said 'she'll take it all' he was referring to Rosalita. It was about Talia. And he was probably right about that."

"And she could have," Beau reminded. "She nearly had Rosalita signing onto anything they asked, using Victor's power of attorney. Rosalita had already given them verbal permission to take ownership of the land for Blue Sage Acres. They did jump the gun a little by sending heavy equipment out there to begin cutting the roads before the property sale actually closed."

"Thank goodness they'd only made a few cuts. Victor was horrified to think his family's land would be divided in such a way and McMansions built out there."

"Oh, Mom, that would have been horrible," Kelly said, passing the deviled eggs around for seconds.

"I know. That parcel of land and his house in town had both been in his family forever. People like Talia just do not understand the depth of people's connection to their ancestral lands out here in the west."

"I meant to ask more about Rosalita," Darryl said. "Never my favorite person, but it seems there is some genuine feeling still between her and Victor?"

Sam shrugged. "I guess. Even though she was under a lot of pressure from Tommy and Talia to use the power of attorney for their gains, and she was about to do it, something in her still cared enough to not reveal where Victor had gone. He told me she was the one who discouraged him from coming home because she was afraid for his safety. He really did get sick over this whole thing, you know. He'd been under so much pressure by last December he couldn't work. Luckily, by the time he escaped their clutches and showed up at his cousin's home in Mexico, the cousin was able to take him in and give him a safe space to rest and recover."

"So, Rosalita wasn't lying about that part." Kelly seemed a little surprised.

"Yeah, I even get the impression they may give their marriage another try. Not sure how that will go," Beau said. "From the stories, they make a somewhat volatile pair. But we'll see."

"It would take me a long time to forgive and forget, if I were in Victor's shoes," Scott added.

Kelly gave him a nudge under the table. "Which you will not ever be, trust me."

Darryl helped himself to another slice of ham as he formulated his next question. "Tommy Barker—what's happening with him? Are there legal charges against him?"

"He could be charged with coercion, and also with abduction for taking Victor to that root cellar and leaving him there. But I get the feeling Victor doesn't want to press charges. He and Tommy used to get along pretty well. I think Victor just wants to put all this behind him and go back to fixing little broken stuff and working in our gardens."

Sam nodded agreement. "That's basically what he told me, too."

"Well, I, for one, cannot wait to see him again and get him out to our place so our garden can start thriving again," said Zoë, raising her glass. "To happy endings."

"Now let's have cake!" Ana reminded.

"To cake!" Scott and Kelly chimed in.

Author notes

First and foremost, I want to thank my editor, Stephanie Dewey, for making this book, and many previous ones, a smoother story than when it began. Stephanie is also the coordinator behind an international beta reader team, each of whom adds her own invaluable contributions. To Eve Osborne, Marcia Koopmann, Susan Gross, Sandra Anderson, Isobel Tamney, Paula Webb, and Gabi Hoffknecht—you have my undying gratitude. Thank you!

Garden Sweets is another of those stories that began with one or two tiny grains of my real-life experience and blossomed forth to something that nowhere nearly resembles the tale of the missing neighborhood gardener I once knew. I'll leave the rest to your imagination.

With the release of this book, I have a little surprise to share. This year, to my writing repertoire, I am adding a new series featuring Emily Plankhurst, the young librarian who has appeared in several of my Samantha Sweet books. Fans may remember her as having a significant role in *The Ghost of Christmas Sweet* and in *Haunted Sweets* (unfortunately, she was not available to attend Kelly's Easter Sunday dinner here in *Garden Sweets*).

For more details about Emily's upcoming adventures and her friendships with the cast of Sam's world, visit my website and subscribe to my newsletter. As the new series develops, I will be unveiling more about what happens as a small-town librarian attracts a series of history-related mysterious happenings, plus a ghost or two!

Thank you for taking the time to read *Garden Sweets*.
If you enjoyed it, please consider telling your friends or
posting a short review. Word of mouth is an author's best
friend and is much appreciated.
Thank you,
Connie Shelton

**There's more coming
for Samantha and family!
In the meantime, if you've missed any…
Turn the page to get the links to all of them.**

Get another Connie Shelton book—FREE! Scan the
QR code to find out how!

Books by Connie Shelton

The Charlie Parker Series
Deadly Gamble
Vacations Can Be Murder
Partnerships Can Be Murder
Small Towns Can Be Murder
Memories Can Be Murder
Honeymoons Can Be Murder
Reunions Can Be Murder
Competition Can Be Murder
Balloons Can Be Murder
Obsessions Can Be Murder
Gossip Can Be Murder
Stardom Can Be Murder
Phantoms Can Be Murder
Buried Secrets Can Be Murder
Legends Can Be Murder
Weddings Can Be Murder
Alibis Can Be Murder
Escapes Can Be Murder
Old Bones Can Be Murder
Sweethearts Can Be Murder
Money Can Be Murder
Road Trips Can Be Murder
Cruises Can Be Murder
Deceptions Can Be Murder
Holidays Can Be Murder - a Christmas novella

The Samantha Sweet Series
Sweet Masterpiece
Sweet's Sweets

Sweet Holidays
Sweet Hearts
Bitter Sweet
Sweets Galore
Sweets Begorra
Sweet Payback
Sweet Somethings
Sweets Forgotten
Spooky Sweet
Sticky Sweet
Sweet Magic
Deadly Sweet Dreams
The Ghost of Christmas Sweet
Tricky Sweet
Haunted Sweets
Secret Sweets
Garden Sweets
Spellbound Sweets – a Halloween novella
Thankful Sweets – A Thanksgiving novella
The Woodcarver's Secret – prequel to the series

The Heist Ladies Series
Diamonds Aren't Forever
The Trophy Wife Exchange
Movie Mogul Mama
Homeless in Heaven
Show Me the Money

Children's Books
Daisy and Maisie and the Great Lizard Hunt
Daisy and Maisie and the Lost Kitten

Sign up for Connie Shelton's free mystery
newsletter at www.connieshelton.com
and receive advance information about new
books, along with a chance at prizes, discounts and
other mystery news!

Contact by email: connie@connieshelton.com
Follow Connie Shelton on Twitter, Pinterest,
Instagram, and Facebook

www.ingramcontent.com/pod-product-compliance
Lightning Source LLC
Chambersburg PA
CBHW020614110726
47899CB00002B/500